PHOENIX - ASHES AND FURY

SREERAM HANUMANTH

Contents

Preface

The pursuit of power is a flame that consumes all in its path—brilliant yet perilous, promising salvation while threatening destruction. In **Phoenix - Ashes and Fury**, this flame is embodied by a mythical phoenix, a creature of unparalleled regenerative power, captured and exploited in a desperate bid to unlock its secrets. But tampering with forces beyond comprehension comes with dire consequences, as the fragile balance between myth and reality collapses.

As the International Rescue Force battles to contain the fallout, they find themselves entangled in a web of ambition, betrayal, and the relentless pursuit of immortality. The world is unprepared for the monsters unleashed—creatures born of legends but shaped by human greed. Yet, the greatest threat may not come from the beasts that now roam the earth, but from the secrets hidden within their creation, and the dark forces pulling the strings.

In a world teetering on the edge of destruction, lines blur between savior and destroyer, hero and monster. What rises from the ashes will not only challenge the boundaries of life and death but force humanity to confront the primal forces it sought to control.

Phoenix - Ashes and Fury is a story of ambition, primal power, and the cost of seeking dominion over the uncontrollable. From the ruins of devastation, something extraordinary may rise—but at what price?

Author's Note

Dear Reader,

Thank you for joining me on the journey through **Phoenix - Ashes and Fury**. This story has been years in the making, born from a passion for the extraordinary and a desire to explore themes of transformation, power, and redemption. Rewriting this world after a decade was as much a personal journey as it was a creative one.

This book is just the beginning of a much larger story, and I hope it sparks the same excitement in you that it did for me while writing it. As a designer and storyteller, I believe stories have the power to transform, and I'm thrilled to share this one with you.

Please note, Phoenix - Ashes and Fury is a work of fiction. The characters, creatures, and events are products of my imagination, and any resemblance to actual people or events is purely coincidental. Some creatures and characters may be inspired by mythology, folklore, or my own creative interpretation.

Thank you for reading, and I look forward to sharing more of this universe with you.

With gratitude,
Sreeram Hanumanth

CHAPTER ONE

EMBERS OF IMMORTALITY

The sun was setting over the city, casting an eerie orange glow across the skyline. Inside the sterile, dimly lit lab of Victor Kane, shadows stretched long across the walls. The faint hum of machinery was the only sound, broken occasionally by the sizzle of an overheating console.

Victor's fingers trembled as they hovered over the syringe on the table. His reflection in the polished surface looked like a ghost—pale, hollow-eyed, veins crawling up his neck like dark vines. Once celebrated as a brilliant scientist, Victor now stood on the edge of desperation. His body, ravaged by a terminal illness, betrayed him.

For years, Victor had pursued the ultimate goal: to cheat death. He had pushed the boundaries of science, bending laws and ethics in his quest to unlock the secrets of immortality. But failure after failure had left him with little more than shattered dreams and a dying body. Now, time had run out.

Victor's eyes shifted to the phoenix in its cage, its golden feathers casting an otherworldly glow in the dim light. The mythical creature had been the key to his final experiment. Its regenerative power was unmatched, a force capable of healing wounds and reversing decay. Victor had spent months extracting its essence, crafting a serum that might save him. But he knew the risks.

Victor whispered to himself, *"I just need more time... just a little more time."*

Behind him, the lab door slid open with a soft hiss, and Mira and Dr. Marcus entered. Mira's sharp gaze swept over the equipment, her lips pressed into a thin line. Marcus adjusted his glasses, his expression one of controlled anxiety.

"Victor," Mira said, her voice cautious but laced with underlying urgency. *"We need to talk."*

Victor didn't look at her. *"I'm busy."*

Victor glanced at the syringe again, his gaze darkening. *"If I wait any longer, I won't make it. But I need more time."*

Mira paused, her voice quiet but purposeful. *"You've spent your life chasing this moment, Victor. I know you. You're not someone who backs down now, not when you've come so far."*

Victor's fingers twitched, hovering over the syringe. His hand was unsteady, doubt creeping in.

"Time's not on your side, Victor," Mira continued, her words now soft, coaxing.

Victor's breath caught as his gaze flickered to her. *"I don't have time for another failure, Mira."*

"You've always been the one who makes the impossible happen. You

can control this—if you think carefully." Her voice was smooth now, almost a whisper. "***Don't let it slip away. You're the only one who can make this work.***"

Victor's resolve wavered. He clutched the syringe, feeling the weight of her words, the weight of his decision. The air in the lab felt thick, suffocating.

With a final, jagged breath, he slammed his hand down on the table, gripping the syringe. "***I can't stop now.***"

Mira nodded slightly, her eyes gleaming with quiet triumph. "***Then let's finish it.***"

Victor didn't respond. His fingers clenched around the syringe, the tremors now steady. He injected the serum into his veins. Pain erupted, intense and blinding, flooding his body with molten heat. His vision blurred, and the lab spun around him.

The phoenix let out a mournful cry, its wings flaring as the golden light from its feathers brightened.

Victor's body contorted violently as the serum took hold. His muscles spasmed, his skin glowing with an unnatural fire.

"***Energy levels spiking!***" Marcus shouted, panic rising in his voice.

"***I'm struggling!***" Victor shouted through clenched teeth, his voice distorted by the transformation. His veins pulsed with molten light as the serum coursed through him.

"***Come on Victor! You can***" Mira cried.

Suddenly, the intercom on the wall crackled to life, startling them all.

"Victor..." The voice was cold, sharp, and commanding. *"Is it ready?"*

Victor froze, his body trembling from the serum's effects. The voice was distant and distorted, filtered through layers of encryption. It wasn't a question—it was a demand. A demand he had grown used to, even if he loathed it.

"I'm finishing it," Victor rasped, barely audible over the sound of the machines.

Before Mira or Marcus could react, the energy in the room surged violently. Sparks erupted from the machines. The phoenix screeched, its wings flaring as the containment field flickered.

"Shut it down!" Mira yelled.

"I can't!" Marcus screamed, his hands frantically tapping at the controls. *"It's overloaded!"*

The lab hummed with an almost deafening roar. Victor's screams joined the chaos as his body twisted uncontrollably. The light from the phoenix blazed so brightly it blinded them all.

And then, with a deafening explosion, the lab erupted in a burst of white-hot light.

Victor screamed.

CHAPTER TWO

THE IRF: SILENT GUARDIANS

The International Rescue Force (IRF), an organization with bases worldwide, including in India, had long been the silent guardians of global peace. Under the leadership of Chief Shaan Raghav, Ashwath's elite team, known for their precision and bravery, had faced the world's darkest threats—terrorism, biochemical weapons, and global hostage crises. Yet nothing could have prepared them for the strange, unbelievable reports that began to surface.

It started with whispers. Isolated incidents of destruction that no conventional weapon could explain. Eyewitness accounts dismissed as hysteria or hallucinations: a creature with wings that ignited the air around it, another that moved so fast it seemed to disappear entirely. These reports were buried, lost in the chaos of global conflict, until the IRF stumbled upon undeniable evidence.

The breakthrough came in the form of a smuggling ring. IRF intelligence intercepted chatter about **"living weapons"** being sold on the black market. Ashwath's team—known for their precision and bravery—was dispatched to investigate a suspected arms deal in a remote coastal city. The mission was clear: locate the smugglers, secure the weapons, and prevent them from falling into the wrong hands.

The team moved in silence as they approached the facility. **Ashwath, their leader**, raised his fist, signaling the group to halt. His sharp gaze swept the perimeter, noting the guards and heavy security. Known for his calm under pressure, Ashwath was the backbone of the IRF's elite squad, and his confidence inspired the same in his team.

"I count six guards," **Irfan** murmured, his voice barely above a whisper. As **second-in-command**, Irfan's tactical mind was unmatched. His ability to assess a situation quickly and plan under pressure had earned him respect, but his calm demeanor often concealed a sharp wit. Even in tense moments, Irfan was known to break the ice with his dry humor—a trait that kept the team grounded when the stakes were high.

"Make it five," **Arjun** said with a smirk, adjusting his position. The **youngest and most impulsive member of the team**, Arjun's energy often bordered on recklessness, but his instincts and quick thinking were undeniable assets.

"Stay focused," **Dr. Priya**, the **team's lead scientist**, interjected as she adjusted her portable scanner. Her calm, analytical voice cut through the tension. While not a soldier, Priya was essential to the mission. Her expertise in biology and experimental tech often gave the team the edge they needed.

At the rear, **Rohit** worked furiously on his tablet, his brow furrowed in concentration. *"Jamming their comms... now,"* he said. As the **team's tech expert**, Rohit's skills in surveillance and hacking were unparalleled. No system was safe from his fingertips, and no mission succeeded without his technical acumen.

"Let's move," Ashwath commanded.

The team breached the facility with precision, clearing the first room and securing the guards. They moved deeper into the warehouse, their weapons raised, expecting to find an arsenal of state-of-the-art firearms. But as they rounded the corner, they froze.

Instead of weapons, they were greeted by rows of massive, reinforced cages. Inside were creatures that defied explanation.

"What... what are those?" Arjun whispered, his voice filled with both awe and fear.

In one cage was a large, serpent-like creature with translucent, shimmering skin that glowed faintly in the dark. Its long body coiled and uncoiled, its emerald eyes tracking every movement. It exhaled with a hiss, sending a cloud of glowing spores into the air that danced in the dim light. In another, a massive wolf-like creature growled low, its glowing blue eyes piercing through the dim light. Its fur crackled with static electricity, the air around it charged with energy.

"That's a Thunderwolf," Dr. Priya murmured, her voice steady but tinged with fascination. *"I've read about these—mystical creature with an innate ability to control electricity. Seeing one alive is... extraordinary."*

Dr. Priya's scanner beeped wildly as she stepped closer, her face a mix of disbelief and fascination. *"These aren't just biological anomalies. They're emitting electromagnetic fields, heat signatures—this isn't normal biology. These are extraordinary creatures."*

"Living creatures being sold as weapons," Irfan muttered, his voice grim. *"What kind of people would do this?"*

Before anyone could answer, a loud crash echoed through the facility. The deal had gone south. One of the buyers, frustrated by delays, had shot a smuggler, triggering chaos. In the commotion, one of the cages malfunctioned, and a creature broke free.

The creature was massive, insect-like, with jagged wings that emitted ultrasonic pulses. The shockwaves shattered glass and disoriented everyone in the room. Guards and buyers scrambled for cover as the beast tore through the facility.

"Engage!" Ashwath barked, his voice cutting through the chaos.

Irfan and Arjun flanked the creature, their weapons drawn. *"It's too fast!"* Arjun yelled as the creature darted toward him, its wings sending another disorienting pulse.

"Rohit, shut those other cages down before we have more problems!" Ashwath ordered, firing a shot that grazed the creature, slowing it momentarily.

"Working on it!" Rohit yelled back, his fingers flying over the tablet.

Suddenly, a group of smugglers charged toward the team, weapons raised. *"We've got company!"* Irfan shouted, ducking behind a crate as bullets ricocheted off the steel walls.

"Priya, stay low!" Ashwath commanded, turning his weapon toward the advancing smugglers. He fired a calculated burst, taking down two as they tried to push forward.

Arjun shifted his focus, firing back at the smugglers while keeping an eye on the creature. *"Irfan, cover me! I'm going for the left flank!"*

"On it!" Irfan replied, popping up from cover to lay down suppressive fire. His shots forced the smugglers to retreat momentarily, giving Arjun the opening he needed to reposition.

Meanwhile, Priya crouched behind a crate, her scanner still in hand. *"It's using soundwaves to attack—target its wings!"* she called out, her voice barely audible over the chaos.

Ashwath nodded sharply, grabbing a sound-dampening grenade from his belt. *"Arjun, Irfan, keep the smugglers off us! Priya, stay on that scanner!"* He hurled the grenade toward the creature, the explosion neutralizing its ultrasonic pulses. The beast staggered, momentarily disoriented.

A smuggler tried to flank Priya, his weapon aimed at her exposed position. Rohit, noticing the threat, pulled his pistol and fired, hitting the smuggler in the leg. *"Stay away from her!"* he shouted, his hands shaking slightly as he returned to the tablet.

"Good shot!" Priya called out, giving him a quick nod before returning to her scanner.

With the creature temporarily neutralized, Ashwath turned his attention back to the smugglers. *"Focus fire on their positions! Keep them pinned!"* he barked, motioning for Irfan to advance.

Irfan grinned despite the chaos, his rifle spitting precision bursts as he moved forward. *"You've got it, boss!"* he said, taking down another smuggler who was reloading too slowly.

"Rohit, any luck with those cages?" Ashwath yelled.

"Almost there!" Rohit replied, furiously typing commands into his tablet. *"Just keep them off me for a few more seconds!"*

As Ashwath and Irfan pushed the remaining smugglers back toward the facility's far end, the creature recovered, letting out a furious screech. It charged toward Arjun, who barely dodged its jagged wings.

"It's up again!" Arjun shouted, rolling behind a fallen crate for cover.

"Keep it distracted!" Ashwath yelled, raising his tranquilizer rifle. He aimed carefully, waiting for the creature to expose a weakness. With a sharp hiss, the dart struck its side. The creature let out a guttural screech, its movements faltering as the tranquilizer began to take effect.

Irfan and Arjun seized the opportunity, flanking the beast and firing additional tranquilizer darts. The creature collapsed, unconscious but still menacing as its jagged wings twitched faintly.

Meanwhile, the last of the smugglers dropped their weapons, surrendering as they realized they were outmatched.

As the dust settled, the team regrouped amidst the wreckage, their breaths heavy. Ashwath nodded. *"Good work. But this is just the beginning. If these creatures are real—and being weaponized—then there's no telling what else is out there."*

The team exchanged grim looks, knowing their mission had taken an unprecedented turn. Mystical creatures, once considered myths, were real. And their existence posed a threat unlike anything the

IRF had ever faced.

"Secure the creatures," Ashwath ordered, motioning toward the unconscious beast and the remaining cages. *"We're taking them back to base."*

Rohit worked quickly, disabling the cage systems entirely while calling in for extraction units. Minutes later, an IRF convoy arrived, equipped with reinforced containment pods designed for biological anomalies.

The unconscious insect-like creature was carefully restrained and loaded into a pod, its jagged wings locked in place by magnetic clamps. The Thunderwolf snarled and snapped but was subdued by an electromagnetic field generator before being guided into another pod. The serpent-like creature coiled defensively, its glowing skin pulsing faintly as it was transferred into a translucent, reinforced chamber.

Priya hovered near the Thunderwolf's pod, her scanner still active. *"The energy it's generating is fascinating,"* she murmured, staring at the crackling sparks across its fur. *"We've never seen anything like this."*

"Save the analysis for later," Ashwath said, his tone brisk. *"Let's get them secured at the base first."*

Back at the IRF headquarters, the creatures were offloaded into high-security containment chambers within the facility's restricted wing. Each chamber was equipped with monitoring systems to ensure the creatures' safety and containment integrity.

The team gathered in the observation room, watching as the creatures settled into their temporary enclosures. The sheer magnitude of what they had discovered weighed heavily on all of them.

"These creatures don't belong here," Priya said softly, breaking the silence. *"We need to find a place where they can exist safely—away from people who would harm or exploit them."*

Ashwath nodded, his expression resolute. *"We're not keeping them here permanently. The IRF is already scouting for an isolated island where they can live freely, without interference. Until then, it's our job to ensure their safety."*

Arjun glanced at the insect-like creature, now resting in its reinforced pod. *"It's strange, isn't it? We came here thinking they were just myths. But seeing them like this... they're not monsters. They're just trying to survive."*

Priya looked at him, her voice filled with conviction. *"That's why we need to protect them. They didn't ask for any of this."*

The team collectively realizing the weight of their mission. Their goal wasn't just to stop those who weaponized these mystical creatures—it was also to ensure that these beings, hunted and exploited, could have a chance to live in peace.

In the aftermath, the IRF leadership couldn't deny the truth any longer. Mystical creatures, once dismissed as myth, were being smuggled, sold, and turned into tools of war. The public, unaware of these dangers, would be unprepared for the devastation they could cause if left unchecked.

Ashwath's team was given an unprecedented mission: to locate and secure not only the smuggled mystical creatures but also those still in the wild, untainted by human greed. Their objective was twofold: to stop those seeking to exploit these creatures as weapons and to protect the remaining ones from falling into the wrong hands. It was unlike anything they'd ever faced before, a mission that would challenge their understanding of the natural and the mythical, and push them to their limits.

Through intensive research, Dr. Priya, the team's lead scientist, discovered a breakthrough. Mystical creatures emitted unique energy signatures—fluctuations in heat, sound, and electromagnetic fields that were unlike anything seen in conventional biology. By modifying the IRF's satellite systems and deploying portable scanners, the team could now track these creatures across the globe.

Their first lead came from intercepted communications pointing to a remote island chain where smugglers had been active. The team prepared for deployment, unsure of what they'd find.

For Ashwath, the mission was personal. These creatures weren't just weapons to him—they were lives that needed protection. But as the team ventured deeper into this strange new world, they began to realize that the smugglers weren't the only ones weaponizing mystical creatures.

Someone far more powerful—and far more dangerous—was pulling the strings behind the scenes.

The IRF had entered uncharted territory, and their mission would test their resolve, their unity, and their humanity like never before.

THE INVISIBLE INFERNO

The IRF gathered in the main briefing hall, a rare assembly of its top operatives and specialists. The usual hum of conversation was replaced by a tense silence, the weight of recent discoveries hanging heavily over the room. At the front, Ashwath stood, his commanding presence filling the space as the digital map behind him flickered to life.

This wasn't just another mission. The IRF, seasoned in tackling the world's most dangerous threats—terrorism, biochemical warfare, rogue governments—was now grappling with something entirely unprecedented: the confirmed existence of mythical creatures.

"Mystical creatures," Ashwath began, his voice steady but carrying a weight the overall team hadn't heard before.

"We've intercepted evidence that suggests they are real. Not only that—they are being weaponized."

The room fell still, the words sinking in slowly. No one spoke. They had dealt with human threats before—terrorists, warlords, and weapons of mass destruction—but the idea of mystical creatures, the kind that were once nothing more than stories and folklore, was a different kind of danger.

The digital map on the wall zoomed in on various locations, red dots appearing on the screen. *"These are confirmed sighting zones,"* Ashwath continued, pointing to the locations scattered across the globe. *"Intelligence suggests these creatures are being captured, smuggled, and sold to mercenaries, rogue states, and private militias. The Phoenix and Kryllis are the most recent reports we've received."*

Dr. Priya, spoke up. *"The Phoenix... It's said to have regenerative abilities that are nearly impossible to counter. And the Kryllis—it's practically a ghost, with the ability to blend into any environment. If they're out there and someone is weaponizing them..."*

"It's not just about taking them down," Ashwath interrupted, his voice firm. *"We need to secure them. These creatures are living beings, and right now, they're being exploited. We can't allow that to happen."*

The team exchanged uneasy glances. The concept of mystical creatures had always been confined to myths—until now.

"This isn't just about recovering smuggled creatures," Ashwath continued, his gaze sweeping across the team. *"We're dealing with an enemy that's more dangerous than any we've faced before. We need to stop the weaponization of these creatures before it's too late."*

Irfan, leaned forward with a grin. *"A Phoenix? I just hope it doesn't get upset and roast us alive. On the bright side, at least we'd go out... well-done."*

A few chuckles rippled through the room, breaking the tension. Irfan's humor, even in the face of danger, was as much a part of their team dynamic as their high-tech weapons. Still, the gravity of the mission wasn't lost on him.

Ashwath allowed himself a brief, tight smile but quickly returned to business. *"This mission isn't like the others. We're not just dealing with mystical creatures—we're dealing with people who know how to weaponize them. I need everyone at full alert. We recover the creatures, secure them, and ensure these creatures doesn't fall into enemy hands. Understood?"*

The team nodded as one, their expressions turning grim. They had encountered dangerous threats before, but none like this. The stakes had never been higher.

Arjun, brow furrowed. *"Understood, but how are we supposed to track these creatures? If they're out there, we don't even know where to begin looking."*

Priya, adjusted her glasses and spoke up. *"Actually, we have a way. Through my research, I've found that mystical creatures give off unique energy signatures. It's like they radiate energy that's different from anything we know in conventional biology. They emit fluctuating heat, electromagnetic fields, and even specific sound frequencies. We've adapted our satellite systems and built portable scanners that can detect these signatures."*

The team exchanged impressed glances. *"So we can track them?"* Irfan asked, his curiosity piqued.

Priya nodded. *"Exactly. Once we're on the ground, we'll be able to pinpoint the creatures' locations. It's not foolproof yet, but it's the best shot we've got."*

Ashwath nodded approvingly. *"That's why we're counting on you, Priya. If anyone can make this work, it's you."*

Priya gave a tight smile, though her eyes remained focused on the task ahead. *"We'll find them, Ashwath. We'll track them down and stop them from being weaponized."*

Ashwath's gaze swept over the room, seeing the determination in each of his team members' eyes. *"Then it's settled. We're going after the Kryllis and the Phoenix. Get ready. We leave in 24 hours."*

The room was filled with the low hum of preparation, each member of the team steeling themselves for what lay ahead. The mission was clear, but the uncertainty of facing creatures no one had ever imagined made the air heavy with tension. Yet they knew one thing for sure—this time, the stakes were higher than ever.

CHAPTER FOUR

WALKING THROUGH THE FIRE

24 Hours later, the team descended from their helicopter into a dense jungle just outside a smuggler's hidden compound. The air was thick with humidity, and the chirping of insects was punctuated by the occasional roar of an unknown creature in the distance.

"I love what they've done with the place," Irfan quipped, pushing a branch out of his way. *"Real cozy."*

"Stay focused," Ashwath snapped, his sharp gaze scanning the perimeter. The uneasy feeling in his chest hadn't eased since they'd arrived. If anything, it had grown stronger.

Dr. Priya, the team's scientist, held up her handheld scanner. The screen pulsed with readings, a blinking red dot marking the location of their first target. *"The Kryllis should be just ahead,"* she said. *"The readings are faint, but it's definitely here."*

The team moved silently through the jungle, their weapons at the ready. As they neared a clearing, the trees gave way to a sprawling compound made of rusted metal and reinforced concrete. Fences lined with electric wiring surrounded the area, and the faint hum of generators filled the air.

"There," Arjun whispered, pointing to a large enclosure near the center of the compound. Through the gaps in the fence, they could see the Kryllis, its crystalline body shimmering faintly as it tried to blend into its surroundings. The creature was massive, easily the size of a small truck, and its jagged scales reflected the moonlight like shards of broken glass.

Ashwath raised a fist, signaling the team to stop. *"We'll split into two groups,"* he said quietly. *"Arjun, Irfan, and Priya, you're with me. Rohit and the rest of you, stay here and cover our retreat. We move fast, secure the Kryllis, and get out. No mistakes."*

As they moved closer to the enclosure, the Kryllis stirred, its glowing eyes locking onto them. It let out a low, rumbling growl, the sound reverberating through the air like distant thunder.

"Easy there, big guy," Irfan muttered under his breath. *"We're here to help, not to get eaten."*

The team reached the enclosure and quickly began disabling the electric fencing. Rohit worked on the control panel while Arjun and Irfan kept watch. Ashwath stood near the entrance, his weapon trained on the compound's main building, watching for any sign of the smugglers.

"We've got movement," Arjun whispered, nodding toward the far side of the compound. Shadows flickered in the distance—guards patrolling the area.

"Stay sharp," Ashwath said, his voice tense. *"Rohit, how much*

longer?"

"Almost there," he replied, his fingers flying over the controls. *"Just a few more seconds."*

The fencing powered down with a soft hum, and the gate swung open. The Kryllis hesitated for a moment, its massive body shimmering as it shifted colors to blend into the jungle behind it. Ashwath stepped forward cautiously, his voice low and steady.

"We're not here to hurt you," he said, addressing the creature directly. *"You're safe now. Let's get you out of here."*

The Kryllis let out another low growl, but it didn't attack. Slowly, it stepped forward, its movements graceful despite its size. The team backed away, giving it space to exit the enclosure.

Suddenly, a shout rang out from the compound. The smugglers had spotted them.

"We've got company!" Arjun yelled, raising his weapon.

Ashwath's instincts kicked in immediately. *"Move! Get the Kryllis to safety!"*

Gunfire erupted as the team sprinted toward the extraction point, the Kryllis following closely behind. Irfan covered their retreat, his sharp aim taking down two of the smugglers who pursued them.

"I told you this place was cozy!" he shouted, grinning as he reloaded his weapon.

"Less talking, more shooting!" Ashwath barked, firing at a guard who had gotten too close.

They reached the helicopter just as the smugglers began closing in. The Kryllis leapt into the cargo hold, its massive form barely fitting inside. The team scrambled aboard, but Ashwath and Arjun hesitated for a split second, knowing they couldn't just leave the smugglers behind.

"Irfan, cover the helicopter!" Ashwath ordered. *"We'll be right back!"*

Irfan nodded, keeping his rifle trained on the approaching smugglers, his finger tight on the trigger. *"Got it! Just don't take too long!"*

Ashwath and Arjun turned back, weapons raised, and sprinted toward the compound. They quickly took cover behind a nearby wall, exchanging fire with the smugglers closing in on them.

Arjun fired, hitting one of the smugglers trying to flank them. *"We can't let them get to the chopper!"* he shouted, ducking as a bullet whizzed past his head.

"I know!" Ashwath growled, taking down another smuggler who was taking aim at them. *"Stay low—let's clear this area and make our way back."*

The two of them moved swiftly, working as a unit to eliminate the remaining smugglers in the immediate area. As the last one fell, Ashwath gave a quick nod.

"Let's go!" Ashwath said, already heading back toward the helicopter with Arjun close behind.

Meanwhile, Irfan stood his ground, covering their retreat. He fired steadily, ensuring no smugglers could get within range of the helicopter. *"Hurry up, you two! I'm not holding this position forever!"*

The team finally reached the helicopter, panting but unharmed. They jumped into the cargo hold, and the door slammed shut just as Irfan sprinted toward it. The rotors roared to life, and the helicopter began to lift off, the jungle falling away below them.

As the helicopter ascended, the smugglers were no longer a threat, their presence fading as the distance between them grew. Irfan exhaled in relief, glancing out the side window as the compound shrank into the distance. *"That was too close,"* he muttered, wiping sweat from his brow.

Ashwath remained silent for a moment, his eyes locked on the horizon, the tension still heavy in his chest. The adrenaline was gone, but something else had settled in its place—a gnawing feeling that this was far from over.

"We got the Kryllis out. That's what matters," he said, his voice calm but with an edge of unease.

Arjun nodded, scanning the horizon as the helicopter gained altitude. *"We got it out. But this isn't over."*

The jungle faded into the distance as the team allowed themselves a brief moment to relax. The Kryllis lay curled in the corner of the cargo hold, its shimmering scales dimming as it settled into a calmer state.

Irfan leaned back against the wall, his body still tense. *"Never thought I'd be taking down smugglers with a mythical creature as backup.*"

Ashwath didn't respond, his gaze still fixed forward. The unease in his chest had grown stronger, not weaker. This was only the beginning.

"Good work, everyone," he said finally, his voice steady but distant. *"But we're not done yet. The Phoenix is still out there."*

CHAPTER FIVE

WHISPERS OF RADIATION

The helicopter's rotors cut through the thick, humid air as it approached Kiltan Island, its once-vibrant tropical beauty now unrecognizable. Below, the landscape was a haunting wasteland of blackened trees, jagged fissures, and faintly glowing patches of scorched earth. Plumes of volcanic smoke spiraled into the darkening sky, casting long shadows over the fractured terrain.

Inside the helicopter, the IRF Team sat silently, each member lost in thought. Ashwath, their leader, leaned forward, his sharp eyes scanning the map displayed on a digital screen. The target location—a mountainous ridge deep in the island—was marked in pulsing red, a warning of the dangers ahead.

Dr. Priya, the team's scientist, studied her handheld scanner, her brow furrowed with concern. *"The radiation levels are... abnormal,"* she said, breaking the silence. *"They're spiking, but the pattern is erratic. It's almost as if the radiation is pulsing."*

"What does that mean?" Irfan asked, leaning forward. *"Are we walking into some kind of sentient energy zone? Because that's definitely above my pay grade."*

Priya shot him a look. *"I'm serious. This isn't normal. Whatever we're dealing with, it's dangerous."*

"And I'm serious too," Irfan replied with a grin. *"If the radiation starts talking, I'm out."*

"Irfan," Ashwath interrupted sharply, his gaze locked on the ridge below. *"Focus. This isn't the time for jokes."*

Irfan straightened, his grin fading, though the playful spark in his eyes remained. *"Understood, Captain. No jokes. Just good old-fashioned danger."*

Beside Ashwath, Arjun sat quietly, his expression unreadable. Though he said nothing, Ashwath could feel the tension radiating from him. They had been through countless missions together, but this one felt different. They both knew it.

"I've never seen anything like this," Priya continued, her voice quieter now. *"It's not just radiation—it's... reactive. Almost like the island itself is responding to something."*

Ashwath's jaw tightened. *"Keep monitoring it. And let's not speculate until we have hard facts."*

The pilot's voice crackled over the comms. *"We're approaching the drop zone. ETA two minutes."*

Ashwath stood, steadying himself as the helicopter tilted slightly. *"Gear up,"* he ordered, his voice calm but firm. *"This isn't just a recovery mission anymore. Whatever's happening here, we need to secure the site and prepare for anything."*

The helicopter landed in a clearing near the edge of the island's dense jungle, its rotors kicking up clouds of ash and debris. The team disembarked quickly, moving in practiced silence. The air hit them immediately—thick, humid, and laced with a faint metallic tang that clung to their lungs.

"This place feels... wrong," Arjun muttered, his eyes scanning the tree line. The jungle was unnaturally quiet, devoid of the usual sounds of life. No birds. No insects. Just an eerie, suffocating silence.

"I don't like it either," Ashwath admitted quietly, though his tone remained steady. *"Stay sharp. Priya, keep an eye on the readings."*

Priya glanced at her scanner, her brow furrowing further. *"The radiation levels are spiking the closer we get to the ridge,"* she said. *"But there's another energy signature coming from the same location. I can't identify it."*

"Fantastic," Irfan muttered, adjusting the strap of his rifle. *"Radiation and mystery energy. Just another day in paradise."*

Ashwath ignored him, motioning for the team to move. *"We'll split into two groups. Arjun, you're with me. The rest of you secure the perimeter. Stay on comms and report anything unusual immediately."*

The team nodded and fanned out, their movements precise and silent. Ashwath led Arjun toward the ridge, the dense jungle giving way to rocky terrain as they climbed higher. The path was treacherous, littered with loose stones and twisted roots, but they moved quickly, their senses on high alert.

CHAPTER SIX

Fallout from the Ashes

As they ascended, the jungle began to thin, and strange markings appeared on the ground. Intricate symbols, etched into the stone, glowed faintly with a soft, otherworldly light.

"What the hell is this?" Arjun asked, crouching to examine one of the symbols.

Ashwath's eyes narrowed as he scanned the markings. *"Not natural. Someone—or something—put this here."*

The symbols pulsed faintly, their glow intensifying as they moved closer to the ridge. The air grew heavier, thick with static energy that made their skin crawl.

When they reached the top, they stopped in unison. Below them, nestled in a shallow valley, was the source of the energy—a massive machine, unlike anything they'd ever seen. Sleek and angular, it pulsed faintly with light, its jagged edges exuding an unsettling hum. Surrounding it were the remains of what appeared to be a lab—broken equipment, scorched metal, and signs of a hurried evacuation.

"This wasn't built by smugglers," Arjun said, his voice low. *"This is something else."*

Ashwath's gaze swept over the area, landing on a cage near the machine. Its bars were twisted and blackened, as though something had melted its way out. Ashes littered the ground around it, and strange symbols similar to those on the ridge were etched into the metal.

"This was for the Phoenix," Ashwath said quietly. *"It's gone. Whatever happened here—it's already out there."*

The faint hum of the machine grew louder as they approached it. Ashwath moved cautiously, inspecting the control panel near its base. The wires were frayed, and sparks danced faintly from exposed circuits.

"It looks like the power's been out for a while," Ashwath said, kneeling down. *"Whoever left here didn't bother fixing it."*

"Or it could've been a short circuit," Arjun replied warily, keeping his distance. *"Either way, let's just secure the area and report back."*

But Ashwath shook his head, his instincts driving him forward. *"We need to know what this thing does. If it's tied to the Phoenix, we can't leave it unchecked."* He began reconnecting wires and testing circuits, his movements methodical despite the growing tension in the air.

"Ashwath, are you sure this is a good idea?" Arjun asked, his voice tense.

"It's better than walking away blind," Ashwath replied, his focus

unwavering. *"Just watch my back."*

As Ashwath worked, the machine sputtered to life, its hum deepening into a low, resonant vibration. The symbols on the cage and surrounding rocks began to glow more brightly, their light pulsing in rhythm with the machine. The air grew heavier, thick with a static charge that made their skin crawl.

"Ashwath," Arjun said, taking a step back. *"I don't think this is—"*

Before he could finish, the machine roared to life. Beams of light shot out from its core, and the ground beneath them began to tremble. Loose rocks tumbled down the slope as the machine emitted a high-pitched whine that pierced the air.

"Ashwath, shut it down!" Arjun shouted, his voice barely audible over the noise.

"I'm trying!" Ashwath yelled back, frantically flipping switches and pulling wires. But it was too late. The machine's energy surged out of control, its light intensifying until it filled the entire valley.

A blinding burst of radiation erupted, flooding the area with searing heat and light. Ashwath and Arjun were caught in its path, their bodies engulfed by the overwhelming energy.

Amid the chaos, a fiery glow filled the room. The Phoenix, hidden in the shadows until now, emerged with a piercing cry. Its golden wings flared brilliantly as it moved between Ashwath and Arjun, its feathers shimmering with an ethereal light.

For a brief moment, the radiation bent around Arjun, its intensity softening. A strange calm washed over him, the searing pain replaced by a fleeting sense of warmth and clarity.

But for Ashwath, there was no such reprieve. His body convulsed, his skin blistering as the energy tore through him. He collapsed to his knees, writhing in agony.

"Ashwath!" Arjun shouted, but his voice was drowned out by the deafening hum of the machine.

The Phoenix let out one last mournful cry before vanishing in a burst of flame, leaving only a faint echo of its presence behind.

When the radiation subsided, the valley was deathly silent. Ashwath lay on the ground, his breathing shallow, his body trembling uncontrollably. Arjun staggered to his feet, disoriented but otherwise unharmed.

"We need to move," Ashwath rasped, his voice barely audible. He tried to stand but faltered, his legs buckling beneath him.

Before Arjun could help him, the ground beneath them began to shift. The radiation had destabilized the ridge, and the rocks above them began to crumble.

"Arjun! Ashwath! Can you hear me?" Irfan's voice crackled through the comms, filled with panic. *"Get out of there—now!"*

"We're trapped!" Arjun shouted, shielding Ashwath as debris rained down around them.

Seconds later, Irfan appeared at the edge of the ridge, his face pale but determined. *"Hold on!"* he yelled, rushing toward them. Dodging falling rocks, he managed to reach them, slinging Ashwath's arm over his shoulder.

"Let's go!" Irfan urged, pulling them both toward safety.

The three of them barely made it out before the ridge collapsed entirely, sending up a plume of dust and ash. They tumbled to the ground outside, coughing and gasping for air.

As they tried to catch their breath, Ashwath's eyes scanned the wreckage, and for a split second, he froze. Among the debris, half-hidden by a pile of rocks, was a broken, discarded piece of equipment—a metal tag. He didn't fully recognize it, but there was something about it, something familiar. The shape, the insignia... Before he could focus on it, his mind grew foggy, his thoughts slipping away like smoke.

"Ashwath?" Arjun's voice broke through his haze. *"What is it? Are you okay?"*

Ashwath blinked, his mind scrambling to latch onto the image that had flashed before him. But it was gone, wiped from his memory as if it never existed. He shook his head, clearing the confusion. *"It's nothing,"* he muttered, forcing himself to his feet. *"Let's just go."*

Ashwath slumped against a rock, his body wracked with tremors. His hands trembled uncontrollably, his breaths coming in shallow, ragged gasps

"What the hell just happened in there?" Irfan demanded, his voice shaking. *"Are you two okay?"*

Arjun glanced at Ashwath, concern etched across his face. *"He's not fine,"* Arjun said quietly. *"We need to get him back to the base."*

Ashwath gritted his teeth, forcing himself to speak. *"I'm fine,"* he said, though the pain in his voice betrayed him. *"We... need to focus on the mission."*

But even as he spoke, something felt off. His body was burning—not from the heat of the radiation but from something deeper, something he couldn't explain. He clenched his fists, his mind clouded with confusion and rage.

"We'll figure this out," Arjun said firmly, his eyes meeting Ashwath's. But as they prepared to leave, Arjun couldn't shake the feeling that whatever had happened in that cave had changed them both—though in very different ways.

The IRF team sat in the briefing room, the tension thick as they reviewed the recordings from Kiltan Island. The images of glowing symbols, the massive machine, and the Phoenix's fiery escape replayed in a loop on the screen. Ashwath stood at the head of the table, arms crossed, his jaw tight.

"This was a disaster," Ashwath said sharply, his voice laced with frustration. *"We went in blind, and now we're left with more questions than answers."*

"We also didn't die," Irfan quipped, leaning back in his chair with a half-smile. *"That's gotta count for something, right? Pretty sure surviving radioactive Phoenix hell earns us a bonus."*

Ashwath's glare cut through the room. *"This isn't a joke, Irfan. We failed."*

Irfan shrugged, unbothered. *"I don't know, boss. I'd say 'not dying' is a solid win. But hey, if you want to dwell on the negative..."*

Priya sighed, adjusting her glasses as she scanned her tablet. *"The readings from the machine are unlike anything we've seen. The radiation wasn't just energy—it seemed reactive, almost... alive. It's possible the Phoenix triggered some kind of response."*

"Yeah, great," Irfan muttered. *"Alive, reactive radiation. Just what we needed. What's next? Sentient lava?"*

"I'm serious, Irfan," Priya replied, her tone calm but firm. *"This isn't a simple incident. The Phoenix's abilities seem to amplify energy around it. If we don't understand how that works, we'll walk into the next mission just as blind."*

Ashwath slammed his hand on the table, silencing the room. *"Then figure it out. We can't afford another failure."*

The team exchanged uneasy glances. Irfan leaned closer to Priya, lowering his voice. *"Someone needs to get him a stress ball. Or a nap."*

Priya shook her head, whispering back, *"I'd recommend a therapist, but I don't think he'd take it well."*

CHAPTER SEVEN

BENEATH THE SMOLDERING SURFACE

The days following the radiation incident were marked by strange and unsettling occurrences. Both Ashwath and Arjun were recovering physically, but it was clear that neither of them had emerged unscathed.

For Ashwath, the change was internal—a growing sense of rage that he could barely contain. He snapped at the team over the smallest things, his patience wearing thin. His once-steady leadership felt overshadowed by a volatile temper, and though he tried to mask it, the tension was palpable.

For Arjun, the changes were more physical. His body healed faster, injuries disappearing within hours. His strength had increased dramatically, and his muscles had become more defined. But it wasn't just physical—he could feel bursts of energy surging through him, leaving him exhilarated but uneasy. It felt like fire coursing through his veins, an energy he couldn't understand or control.

Late one night, Ashwath sat alone on the observation deck, staring out at the vast expanse of stars. His jaw was tight, his fists clenched. The quiet should have been calming, but instead, it felt suffocating.

He heard footsteps behind him but didn't turn around. *"What do you want, Arjun?"*

Arjun hesitated before stepping forward. He had noticed Ashwath's erratic behavior lately, but he didn't know how to approach it. *"Just checking in. You've been... different since the island."*

"I'm fine," Ashwath said curtly, though his tone lacked conviction.

"You don't look fine," Arjun pressed. *"You've been on edge, snapping at everyone. What's going on?"*

Ashwath finally turned to face him, his gaze cold and distant. *"I said I'm fine, Arjun. Just focus on the mission."*

Arjun studied him, searching for any sign of the man he had always looked up to. *"Look, if something's wrong, you can tell me. We're a team."*

For a moment, Ashwath's expression softened, but the flicker of vulnerability was gone as quickly as it appeared. *"I'll be fine once we finish this,"* he said, his voice quieter but no less tense.

But even as he spoke the words, Ashwath knew they weren't true. Whatever was happening to him—it was growing, consuming him from the inside out.

Later that evening, Arjun found himself in the infirmary, staring at his reflection in the polished metal of a cabinet. His hands clenched and unclenched involuntarily, a faint glow pulsing beneath his skin for the briefest of moments. The changes were undeniable now, but he still didn't understand them.

"Careful, you'll crack that mirror," Irfan's voice broke the silence, his usual humor cutting through the tension.

Arjun turned to see Irfan leaning casually against the doorway, arms crossed, a grin tugging at the corners of his mouth. *"What's going on with you, man? You've been acting weird since Kiltan."*

Arjun hesitated. He trusted Irfan—he was his best friend, the one person who could always make him feel grounded. If there was anyone he could confide in, it was him.

"Irfan..." Arjun began, his voice hesitant, almost trembling. *"Something's... different. After the island, I started noticing things."*

"Noticing things?" Irfan asked, raising an eyebrow, his usual humor masking a flicker of concern. *"What kind of things?"*

Arjun sighed, running a hand through his hair, his frustration evident. *"I heal faster now. My strength—it's unnatural, like I could tear through steel without even trying. But that's not all."*

The humor faded from Irfan's face, replaced by genuine unease. *"What else, Arjun? What aren't you telling me?"*

Arjun stepped closer, lowering his voice as if afraid of being overheard. *"There's this... energy inside me. It doesn't just feel like fire—it is fire. It's alive, and it's growing. And it's not just inside me. Sometimes I feel like it wants out."* His hands trembled slightly as he clenched them into fists. *"I'm afraid to even try controlling it."*

Irfan stared at him, the silence stretching uncomfortably. His eyes scanned Arjun's face, searching for any trace of the friend he knew. *"Arjun..."* he said finally, his voice quieter now. *"Are you saying you're... changing?"*

"I don't know what I'm saying!" Arjun snapped, taking a step back. *"I don't know what's happening to me! Sometimes it feels like I'm losing control, like... like something else is taking over. I'm scared, Irfan."*

For once, Irfan didn't crack a joke. His shoulders stiffened, and he looked at Arjun with something close to fear. *"Okay. Whatever this is, we'll figure it out. But, Arjun..."* He hesitated. *"You're not... hurting anyone, right?"*

Arjun's jaw tightened, his expression darkening. *"Not yet,"* he said, his voice low. *"But I don't know how much longer I can hold it back."*

The weight of his words hung heavy in the air. Irfan forced a tight smile, trying to inject some reassurance. *"We'll deal with this. Together. Just... promise me, if things start going bad, you'll tell me. Don't let it get to a point where I can't help you."*

Arjun nodded reluctantly, though his eyes betrayed his doubt. *"Thanks, Irfan."*

Irfan took a step back, his usual humor forced. *"Sure thing. But if you start growing claws or glowing eyes, I'm out. No offense, bro."*

Arjun chuckled dryly, though the tension in his chest didn't ease. Deep down, he feared the worst—that he was already slipping away from who he used to be.

As Irfan watched Arjun walk away, his mind couldn't help but wander back to the radiation incident on Kiltan Island. Could this be a delayed effect? The radiation had been unlike anything they'd encountered before, and Arjun's strange new abilities... Irfan wasn't sure what to believe. Could it be that Arjun was just hallucinating, his mind playing tricks on him because of the exposure? The more Irfan thought about it, the more uncertain he became. Still, he kept the thought to himself for now. Whatever was happening to Arjun, Irfan knew they couldn't ignore it any longer. He just hoped they could figure it out before things got worse.

Later that night, Arjun found himself standing outside Taara's door, his fists clenched tightly at his sides. The soft glow of the hallway light flickered above him, casting long shadows that seemed to mirror the turmoil within. He hadn't seen her since the mission on Kiltan Island, and the weight of everything he'd been carrying was becoming unbearable.

Taking a deep breath, Arjun raised his hand and knocked lightly. A few moments passed before the door creaked open, revealing Taara's familiar face. Her eyes widened slightly in surprise before softening into a warm, relieved smile.

"*Arjun,*" she said, stepping aside to let him in. "It'***s been a while. I was starting to worry.*"

Arjun entered hesitantly, his shoulders tense. The small apartment felt comforting, filled with reminders of Taara's personality—photos on the walls, soft lighting, and a faint scent of jasmine. He hadn't realized how much he missed the sense of normalcy she brought until now.

"*I'm sorry,*" Arjun said, his voice low. "*I should've come sooner.*"

She waved his apology away, guiding him to the couch. "You're here now. That's what matters. What's going on?"

Arjun sat down, his hands clasped tightly as he struggled to find the words. *"Something's wrong, Taara,"* he finally said, his voice cracking slightly. *"I don't even know how to explain it."*

Taara perched on the armrest beside him, concern etched across her face. *"What do you mean?"*

"After the mission on Kiltan Island..." Arjun hesitated, his gaze dropping to his hands. *"Something happened to me. My body—it's not the same. There's this... energy inside me. It feels like fire, like it's alive. I don't know what it is, and it scares me."*

Taara stared at him, her brows furrowing slightly as she processed his words. The silence stretched for a moment, and Arjun braced himself for the worst—for fear, for rejection, for disbelief.

But instead, she reached out, placing a hand on his. Her touch was steady and reassuring. *"Arjun,"* she said firmly, *"you're still you. Whatever's happening, we'll figure it out. You don't have to go through this alone."*

Her words caught him off guard, easing the knot of tension that had been growing in his chest. *"You really think so?"* he asked, his voice barely above a whisper.

"I know so," she replied, her expression resolute. *"You've always been strong, Arjun. Whatever this is, it doesn't define you. We'll face it together."*

As she spoke, Taara couldn't shake the feeling that Arjun was simply worn out. His continuous missions, the stress, and now this strange new ability—it all seemed to be piling up. She could see the exhaustion in his eyes, the toll it was taking on him. She knew he was struggling, not just with the changes, but with the weight of everything he had to face. But in that moment, she knew he needed support more than anything.

For the first time in days, Arjun felt a flicker of hope. *"Thanks, Taara,"* he said, his voice steadier now. *"I just... I needed to tell someone. I couldn't keep this to myself anymore."*

"I'm glad you did," she said softly, her eyes meeting his. *"Just promise me you'll be careful."*

"I promise," Arjun said, a faint smile tugging at the corners of his lips.

The two sat there for a moment longer, the weight of the world feeling just a little lighter. In Taara's presence, Arjun felt grounded, as though he could face whatever was coming next. Yet, even with that grounding, the fire within him still burned. For the first time, it didn't feel like something to fear. It felt like something he could control—and maybe even use. But as much as he tried to convince himself, he couldn't shake the feeling that the answers he sought were still out of reach. He knew he had to find them—before the fire consumed him completely.

CHAPTER EIGHT

WHEN FLAMES BREAK FREE

The first monster attack came swiftly, tearing through the fragile peace the city had clung to. Streets once alive with bustling activity were now scenes of devastation, marked by crumbling buildings and infernos raging out of control. Screams of terror echoed as the monstrous creature rampaged, its sheer size and uncontrollable strength reducing everything in its path to ruins. The team had faced threats before, but nothing like this—this was beyond comprehension, beyond reason.

"Move out!" Ashwath barked, urgency cutting through the chaos. His sharp tone left no room for hesitation.

Ashwath had always been a pillar of calm in the storm, but now, his words carried a simmering anger that made the team uneasy. It was as if the destruction around them mirrored the turmoil brewing within him.

As the team mobilized, their attempts to contain the creature felt futile. The monster was relentless, its blows shattering defenses and tossing debris into the air like leaves in the wind. Each of its roars shook the ground, a deafening reminder of the hopelessness of their situation.

But amidst the chaos, one question lingered like a shadow over their efforts: Where was Arjun?

"Irfan, eyes on Arjun?" Priya called, glancing at her tracker.

"Nothing. He's offline," Irfan snapped, scanning the wreckage. *"Damn it, where is he?"*

"Focus on the target!" Ashwath shouted, cutting through Irfan's frustration. *"We can't afford distractions."*

The words stung, but the team had no time to dwell on them. Ashwath charged toward the creature, his movements aggressive, almost reckless. His usual precision had been replaced with raw, unrelenting fury. He attacked with a ferocity that startled even his closest allies. The monster seemed to respond in kind, growing more ferocious with every clash, as though it were feeding off Ashwath's anger.

"Ashwath, fall back!" Priya called out, concern evident in her voice. But Ashwath ignored her, his focus fixed solely on the creature.

Meanwhile, Irfan's concern for Arjun only grew. *"Something's not right,"* he said, gripping his weapon tightly. *"He wouldn't just disappear like this."*

"We don't have time for this," Ashwath snapped, his tone harsher than anyone had expected. He delivered another devastating blow to the monster, forcing it to stagger back momentarily.

When the creature finally retreated, its massive form disappearing into the smoke and rubble, the team was left standing amidst the destruction. Fires crackled, the air thick with smoke and ash, as they tried to regroup. But even as they caught their breath, the absence of Arjun loomed over them like a dark cloud.

"I don't understand," Irfan said, his voice quieter now, filled with unease. He stared at the devastation around him, his shoulders heavy with doubt. *"Arjun should have been here. He wouldn't just leave us like this. Where did he go?"*

Ashwath's jaw tightened as he surveyed the ruined city. *"We'll find him,"* he said tersely. His voice carried no reassurance, only an edge of irritation. *"Right now, secure the area. Focus on the civilians."*

But even as he barked orders, Ashwath's mind was a whirlwind of conflicting thoughts. The destruction wasn't random; it was deliberate, calculated. The way the creature moved, the targets it chose—it wasn't just an attack. It was personal.

A nagging suspicion gnawed at the back of his mind, one he couldn't shake no matter how hard he tried. Could Arjun be connected to this? Could his absence mean something more than just bad timing?

Ashwath clenched his fists, his anger bubbling to the surface again. *"We'll deal with it,"* he muttered under his breath. But even he wasn't sure if he meant finding Arjun or confronting the growing doubts consuming him.

For now, the team sifted through the ruins, their spirits weighed down by the destruction left in the monster's wake. And though no one voiced it, the question lingered in every mind: Was the real monster closer to home than they dared to believe?

CHAPTER NINE

THE SEARCH: THROUGH ASH AND EMBER

The aftermath of the first monster attack left the team shaken, but for Irfan, Arjun's absence weighed heavier than the destruction they had witnessed. Arjun had always been the one who showed up, no matter the odds. His sudden disappearance wasn't just strange—it was unthinkable.

Irfan couldn't shake the feeling that something was wrong. He dove into every scrap of information he could find, combing through mission logs, surveillance footage, and tracking data in a desperate bid to locate his missing teammate.

He remembered the conversation he'd had with Arjun after the mission on Kiltan Island. Arjun had mentioned feeling different, stronger, like something was changing inside him. At the time, Irfan had brushed it off, chalking it up to the aftereffects of the radiation. He hadn't taken it seriously. But now, with everything that had happened—the monster attack, Arjun's disappearance—he couldn't help but wonder if those changes weren't just a side effect of the radiation. He had dismissed his friend's warning too easily, and now, he feared the consequences.

Irfan sat in the dimly lit command room, the faint glow of his laptop casting sharp shadows on his face. The screen displayed surveillance footage from the most recent attack, the creature's hulking form rampaging through the city. His finger hovered over the pause button as he stared at the frame, his gut twisting.

The monster's movements felt eerily familiar—almost human. The way it recoiled from a blow, the way it turned toward the chaos, as if deciding its next target. Irfan leaned back in his chair, rubbing his temples.

"This doesn't make sense," he muttered under his breath. **"It shouldn't feel like..."** He trailed off, unwilling to finish the thought.

A knock at the door startled him. Priya entered, her brow furrowed. **"Still working?"**

"Yeah," Irfan said, quickly closing the laptop. **"Just... trying to make sense of it all."**

She studied him, her analytical gaze sharp. **"You've been quiet since the attack. What's going on?"**

"Nothing," he said, his tone clipped. But the hesitation in his voice betrayed him.

Priya tilted her head. **"You're a terrible liar, Irfan. If you think you've found something, you need to share it."**

Irfan sighed, his shoulders slumping. **"It's just... the way the creature looked. It's powers. It reminded me of someone."**

"Who?" Priya pressed.

Irfan hesitated, his stomach knotting. *"Arjun."*

Priya's eyes widened, but she said nothing. Irfan continued, his voice quieter now. *"I don't want to believe it. He's my best friend, but... he's been different since Kiltan. When he told me about the changes he was feeling, I just thought it was the radiation effect. But now, for the first time, he's missing right when this monster shows up."*

Priya placed a hand on his shoulder. *"If you're right, then we need to find him. Before it's too late."*

Irfan nodded, his jaw tightening. *"I just hope I'm wrong."*

Determined to uncover the truth, Irfan turned his attention back to the tracking systems. He began cross-referencing Arjun's last known locations with recent activity logs. Using the surveillance feeds and mission records, he traced Arjun's movements back to where the first attack had started. The trail was faint but clear—it led to the outskirts of the city, close to where the monster was first spotted.

"Arjun, what are you hiding?" Irfan muttered as he followed the trail on his screen. *"Why didn't you tell me?"*

Later that evening, Irfan called Taara.

"Taara," he said when she picked up, her voice laced with worry. *"I need to ask you something important."*

"Yes, Irfan, all good?" she replied, her voice tinged with concern.

"No," Irfan admitted, his throat tightening. *"Arjun is missing. He hasn't been responding, and I need to know—when he came to see you, did he say anything else? Anything... unusual?"*

Taara hesitated, and when she spoke, her voice was quiet. *"He said something had changed. He talked about this energy inside him, like fire, and how it scared him. Why are you asking me this?"*

Irfan's grip on the phone tightened. *"Did he mention losing control? Did he seem dangerous?"*

Taara's voice broke slightly. *"He said he could barely control it, but he wasn't dangerous, Irfan. He was just... afraid. He didn't know what was happening to him."*

Irfan clenched his jaw, the pieces falling into place in a way he didn't want to believe. *"Taara,"* he said carefully, *"if you hear from him—if he contacts you—promise me you'll tell me immediately. No matter what."*

"Irfan, what's going on?" she asked, her voice trembling. *"Do you think... do you think he's the monster?"*

Irfan hesitated, his silence speaking volumes. *"I don't know,"* he said finally. *"But I need to find him before it's too late."*

In her apartment, Taara sat in stunned silence after the call ended. The idea that Arjun could be connected to the monster attacks was unthinkable. She clutched her phone tightly, her thoughts a whirlwind of fear and confusion.

"Come back, Arjun," she whispered into the empty room, her voice

trembling. *"Please."*

The next morning, Irfan returned to his laptop, poring over the team's mission data once again.

He leaned back in his chair, staring at the screen. If his suspicions were right, then finding Arjun wasn't just about bringing him home—it was about stopping him from becoming something they couldn't control.

"I hope I'm wrong," Irfan whispered. *"But if I'm not..."* He didn't finish the thought.

CHAPTER TEN

THE SILENT FURY

The IRF had received crucial intel that a Basilisk—a creature from ancient lore, said to possess a deadly gaze that could turn anyone to stone—was being smuggled into a remote location. Ashwath's team was assigned to intercept and secure the creature before it could be used as a weapon. But this mission felt different. Ashwath could feel the weight of it in the pit of his stomach—a heaviness he couldn't explain.

No sooner had the team located the smuggling hideout in a dilapidated warehouse on the outskirts of the city than Ashwath's instincts took over. The mission required precision, but a growing frustration simmered within him, his body wound tight like a spring ready to snap. Without consulting his team or waiting for the full plan, Ashwath moved.

In the blink of an eye, he was a shadow in motion. His body flowed through the gaps in the perimeter, faster than the guards could react. The wind seemed to follow him as he moved across the open ground, each step deliberate and almost inhuman in its speed. By the time the guards reached for their weapons, Ashwath had already incapacitated two with silent, lethal force. He moved with surgical precision, taking them down with swift, efficient blows—no hesitation, no wasted motion.

The remaining guards didn't stand a chance. Ashwath's fury masked any signs of vulnerability as he took down the rest of the smugglers in quick succession. His actions were cold, brutal—a force of nature that seemed unstoppable.

The team, still stationed outside, had no idea what was happening. Irfan, Priya, and Rohit waited in tense silence, unaware that Ashwath had already neutralized the entire guard team. When they heard the final crash of a body hitting the ground, they rushed in, weapons drawn.

They found Ashwath standing alone in the middle of the warehouse, surrounded by the unconscious smugglers. His breath came in steady, controlled bursts. The Basilisk's cage stood nearby, its occupant still inside, unaware of the chaos that had just unfolded.

Irfan's eyes widened as he took in the scene. *"What the hell, Ashwath? We were supposed to take them down together. Why did you go in alone?"*

Ashwath didn't respond immediately. His face was unreadable, his gaze cold and focused on the cage, but there was something about him that felt... off. Irfan's voice, tinged with frustration, cut through the tension.

"You just went in there without any backup, without a plan," Irfan pressed, trying to make sense of the uncharacteristic behavior. *"What happened to waiting for us?"*

Ashwath's eyes flicked toward Irfan, but he didn't answer. The silence stretched between them like a chasm, thick with unspoken words. The usual calm leader had become something else—something harder, more detached.

"Focus on the mission," Ashwath finally muttered, his tone blunt, cutting through the conversation. His voice held no warmth, no hint of the leader the team had always relied on.

Irfan stood there, his frustration mounting. *"This isn't like you. You're not even listening to me, Ashwath. We need to be a team."*

Ashwath didn't respond. Instead, he walked toward the cage holding the Basilisk, his steps measured and deliberate, like nothing had happened. The others exchanged uneasy glances but remained silent, unsure of how to address the unsettling change in their leader.

Irfan stepped forward, voice low, almost a whisper. *"What's really going on with you?"*

But Ashwath was already moving again, his eyes fixed on the creature, his mind clearly elsewhere.

CHAPTER ELEVEN

SHADOWS OF THE BEAST

Days passed, but Arjun remained missing. Despite their best efforts, the team couldn't locate him. The sense of dread had grown, and Ashwath found himself spiraling. The anger inside him was becoming harder to control. Every time he thought of Arjun, a wave of anger surged through him, clouding his thoughts. His body felt like a pressure cooker, ready to explode at any moment. He couldn't shake the feeling that something much worse than just a missing person was at play.

Then, as if on cue, a second attack took place—more violent and destructive than the first. The team was summoned into action once again, and this time, Ashwath took the lead with a cold, unyielding determination. The air felt thick with tension as they approached the wreckage. The monster's trail was more scattered this time, but the damage was unmistakable. The scene was eerily similar to the first attack, but Ashwath couldn't shake the nagging sensation that something was off. Something about the destruction felt different, more calculated.

"This isn't just another random monster," Ashwath muttered, his eyes scanning the wreckage. **"Someone's orchestrating this. Someone's pulling the strings."** He clenched his fists, trying to rein in the fury that was rising within him. He could feel the darkness that was slowly creeping over him, threatening to take control.

Irfan glanced at Dr. Priya, his face furrowed with concern. *"Do you think it's the same creature? Or is it something... more?"*

Dr. Priya shook her head, biting her lip. *"It doesn't make sense. The patterns aren't adding up. Whatever this is... it's evolving."*

"Evolving?" Irfan snorted. *"Fantastic. We've gone from bad to worse. Next thing you know, it'll be applying for citizenship."*

"Not the time, Irfan," Priya muttered, adjusting her scanner as it beeped frantically. *"The electromagnetic pulses are irregular. It's as if the creature is testing its surroundings."*

Ashwath's hands were shaking as he pointed to the destruction around them. *"It's not just evolving. It's planned. Someone's making this happen."* His voice was tight, his usual calm demeanor now replaced with a barely-contained rage.

Irfan raised an eyebrow. *"So, what? We've got some evil mastermind training these things? I've seen this movie, and it doesn't end well."*

"Focus, Irfan!" Ashwath snapped, his voice cutting through the tension like a blade. *"This ends now."*

As they moved deeper into the wreckage, Ashwath's temper began to fray. His commands were sharper, his patience non-existent. He barked orders, his voice growing harsher with each passing moment.

Priya crouched by a fallen wall, her voice calm as she called out, *"The creature's movement pattern is erratic, but there's a clear path through the debris. It's targeting specific structures—high density areas. If we don't act fast, it'll move toward the center of the city."*

"Great," Irfan muttered, ducking as a chunk of debris fell nearby. *"Because what we needed was a monster with strategy. Anything else we should know? Maybe it plays chess?"*

Ashwath spun toward him, his glare icy. *"If you're done joking, maybe you could help."*

"Sure thing, boss." Irfan smirked, lifting his rifle. *"But if this thing starts spouting Shakespeare, I'm calling for backup."*

The creature roared, sending a shockwave through the air. Priya's scanner beeped wildly. *"Its pulses are intensifying—watch out for electrical surges!"* she shouted.

Irfan groaned. *"Great. A monster and a walking EMP. What's next? It starts hacking into our comms?"*

"Enough!" Ashwath barked. *"We take it down now."*

"But—" Priya started, her voice steady but concerned.

"No," Ashwath growled. *"No more waiting. We stop it, or more people die."*

The tension between them hung in the air, but Priya nodded reluctantly, her grip tightening on her scanner.

The fight that followed was brutal. The creature moved with a calculated ferocity, its glowing eyes tracking their every move. Irfan cracked nervous jokes between shots, while Priya calmly called out scientific observations, trying to guide Ashwath's increasingly aggressive attacks.

"We need to regroup!" Priya yelled as the creature struck a nearby building, sending debris raining down.

"There's no time!" Ashwath snarled, firing relentlessly. His movements were precise but fueled by a barely-contained fury that frightened even his closest allies.

Irfan exchanged a worried look with Priya as they scrambled for cover. *"He's not himself, is he?"*

"No," Priya said quietly, glancing at Ashwath as he charged forward. *"There's something wrong with him. He's pushing himself too hard. And I think he's pushing all of us too hard, too."*

Finally, the creature let out a deafening roar and retreated into the smoke, leaving behind a trail of destruction. The team was left standing amidst the wreckage, exhausted and shaken.

Irfan broke the silence, his voice unusually subdued. *"We need to find Arjun. Whatever's happening, we need him back. He's the key to all of this. He's the one who can help us make sense of this."*

The rest of the team nodded in agreement, their expressions a mix of frustration and uncertainty. The longer Arjun remained missing, the more their suspicions grew. There were too many unanswered questions—too many inconsistencies—and they all pointed to Arjun. But where was he?

Ashwath stood apart from the group, his gaze fixed on the horizon. His posture was rigid, his hands clasped tightly behind his back. He hadn't spoken much since the latest attack, and his silence was unsettling. The others had noticed it too. Normally the team could rely on him for clear guidance, but now he seemed distant, his mind elsewhere.

Flashbacks of the overwhelming radiation flashed through his mind. Every time he tried to focus on the memories, they slipped away, leaving him with an unsettling sense of confusion. His jaw tightened, but he kept the thought to himself.

Finally, Ashwath turned to face them. His expression was unreadable, his eyes hollow with a strange intensity. *"I need to leave,"* he said abruptly, his voice flat, devoid of emotion.

The team froze. Irfan stepped forward, his face a mixture of confusion and disbelief. ***"What do you mean, leave? Ashwath, we need you here. You're the one keeping us together. Without you, we—"***

Ashwath's eyes flicked to Irfan, a fleeting flicker of something—pain, anger, confusion?—crossing his face before he turned away. *"I have to figure something out,"* he said, his voice tight. *"Something that can't wait."*

Irfan took a step closer, his brow furrowed. ***"Is this about Arjun? About... all of this?"*** His voice lowered, uncertain.

Ashwath paused for a moment, his face expressionless, before replying with a cold, finality that sent chills down Irfan's spine. ***"Don't look for me,"*** he said firmly. ***"Stay focused on the mission. I'll be back when I have answers."***

The silence that followed was deafening. The rest of the team exchanged uneasy glances, their trust in Ashwath making it difficult to question his decision. But Irfan couldn't help but feel a sense of foreboding, a nagging feeling that Ashwath was hiding something from them.

"You're not making sense, Ashwath. If this is about Arjun, we should be working together, not splitting up," Irfan said, his voice rising with frustration.

Ashwath's gaze flicked to Irfan, his eyes steely. *"Trust me on this,"* he said, his voice quiet but laced with an edge of authority. *"I'll be back with answers. But for now, I have to go."*

Without another word, Ashwath turned and walked away, his footsteps heavy and deliberate. The team watched him go, their faces a mixture of confusion and concern. None of them could fully grasp what Ashwath was going through, but they knew one thing: he was slipping away from them.

Irfan exhaled sharply, running a hand through his hair in frustration. *"He's trying to figure out what's happening with Arjun,"* he said finally, his voice thick with doubt. *"And honestly... I get it. Whatever's going on out here, it's bigger than all of us. But we need answers. Fast."*

The team nodded hesitantly, though unease rippled through the group. Ashwath's departure left a void they weren't sure how to fill. The weight of his absence was palpable, and it felt like the threads of their unity were beginning to unravel.

Irfan stood still for a moment, staring at the spot where Ashwath had disappeared. *"Come back with those answers,"* he muttered under his breath. *"We're running out of time."* He turned back toward the team, determination hardening his features. *"We have a mission. Let's focus on that. Arjun is out there, and we will find him. We have no choice."*

With one last glance toward the horizon, Irfan led the team forward, each step filled with uncertainty, but the lingering question of Ashwath's departure echoing in their minds.

As the days dragged on without any sign of Arjun, the weight of his absence bore heavily on the team. Each passing moment without answers deepened their unease, especially as monster attacks grew more violent and frequent. Irfan couldn't shake the gut-wrenching feeling that Arjun's disappearance and the attacks were tied to something far more sinister—a larger plan unfolding in the shadows.

Ashwath's departure had left a void in the team's leadership, making their struggle even harder. Despite the mounting challenges, they had no choice but to press on. Every monster attack brought new devastation, and though they pieced together fragments of evidence, the clues only seemed to lead them in frustrating circles.

Meanwhile, there were whispers about Kryllis—an unsettling silence surrounding it as it was moved to an international base, far from the chaos of the IRF headquarters. Irfan had heard the rumors, but with everything happening around him, he couldn't afford to think too much about it. His focus remained squarely on finding Arjun and stopping the escalating attacks. The strain of the mission was overwhelming, and there was simply no time to divert his attention elsewhere.

For Irfan, the mission became deeply personal. Arjun wasn't just a teammate—he was his best friend. That bond fueled Irfan's determination to uncover the truth, even as his concerns for Arjun grew darker. He couldn't ignore the nagging questions: Where was Arjun? And could he still be the person Irfan knew, or had something changed him irreversibly?

The team felt the strain of Ashwath's absence. Without his steady command, tensions began to rise, and their once-unified purpose felt fractured. Irfan and Priya carried on, driven by duty and desperation, but the cracks in their resolve became harder to ignore. The longer Arjun remained missing, the more their focus wavered, caught between the escalating chaos of the mission and the looming fear that they might be running out of time to bring him back.

CHAPTER TWELVE

THE TRANSFORMATION AWAITS

The night enveloped Victor's mansion like a shroud, its grand structure crumbling from years of abandonment and the chaos of illegal experiments. Inside, the faint moonlight crept through broken windows, illuminating the eerie stillness. A shadow slipped into the ruins, moving with both urgency and unease.

The intruder—silent, focused—navigated the wreckage, his boots crunching against shattered glass. His movements were sharp, purposeful, but there was a tremor in his hands, a slight hesitation in his steps. He wasn't here for vengeance. Not yet. He was searching for something.

The air inside the mansion was heavy, almost suffocating, as though the walls themselves were holding their breath. The man's eyes darted across the room, scanning over scattered files, overturned tables, and remnants of Victor's experiments. Strange equipment, shattered glass tanks, and scorched floors hinted at the horrors that had taken place here.

He rifled through drawers, throwing aside useless documents, his breathing growing heavier. Whatever he was looking for, it wasn't here—or perhaps, it was hidden deeper. His frustration mounted, and as he reached for a locked metal case on the far side of the room, a sudden wave of dizziness overtook him.

He staggered, clutching his chest, the case forgotten. His body stiffened, his muscles tightening painfully. The intruder dropped to his knees with a guttural gasp, his hands trembling violently.

His veins glowed faintly beneath his skin, burning like molten fire. His muscles rippled, his body contorting in ways that defied human limits. The pain was excruciating, every nerve in his body aflame. His nails elongated into razor-sharp claws, and his teeth sharpened into fangs. A low growl escaped his throat, distorted and primal.

The mansion seemed to respond to his agony. The air crackled with energy, and the cages holding Victor's past experiments rattled violently, as if the creatures within could sense what was happening.

With a roar that shook the walls, the man slammed his hand into the ground, leaving deep claw marks on the marble floor. Flames erupted from his body, uncontrolled and wild, spreading quickly to the surrounding debris. The heat intensified, and the fire licked hungrily at the curtains, the furniture, and the walls.

The intruder's glowing eyes snapped to a shattered mirror across the room. What he saw made him recoil—a creature, monstrous and unrecognizable, stared back at him. His mind was still human, but his body had become something else entirely.

"*No... no...*" he muttered, his voice deep and guttural, barely audible over the crackling flames. "***This can't be me.***"

But the creature inside him roared louder, drowning out his thoughts. The fire spread, engulfing the room in an inferno. The mansion groaned under the pressure, beams collapsing as the heat weakened the structure.

The flames consumed the mansion entirely.

CHAPTER THIRTEEN

DARKNESS BENEATH THE BLAZE

The IRF team arrived at Victor's mansion to find chaos unfolding. Flames leapt into the night sky, illuminating the crumbled remains of what had once been a symbol of grandeur. The acrid scent of burning debris filled the air as the team quickly fanned out to assess the destruction.

"Irfan, what's the call?" Priya asked, her voice strained over the crackling of the flames.

Irfan, now leading the mission in Ashwath's absence, surveyed the scene with narrowed eyes. *"We secure the area. Watch for any movement. Whatever did this... it's still out there."*

The team moved cautiously through the smoldering wreckage, their weapons drawn. The mansion's interior was unrecognizable—walls collapsed, furniture splintered, and claw marks gouged deep into the marble floors.

"This wasn't just a rampage," Rohit muttered, running his hand over one of the marks. *"This thing tore through here with purpose."*

A low growl echoed from the shadows, cutting through the crackle of the fire. Irfan froze, his heart pounding as he motioned for the team to stay silent. The growl grew louder, closer. Then, from the smoke, the monster emerged.

It was enormous, its hulking form barely discernible through the flickering flames. Its glowing eyes burned with an intensity that made Irfan's breath hitch. The way it moved—deliberate, almost calculated—sent a chill down his spine. It felt familiar, like watching a distorted reflection of someone he knew.

"Hold your ground!" Irfan barked, raising his weapon.

The monster lunged without warning, its speed defying its massive size. Irfan fired, his bullets finding their mark but barely slowing the creature. It roared in pain, swiping at him with claws that sliced through the wreckage like paper. Irfan dodged, landing a hit to its shoulder, drawing blood that hissed as it hit the ground.

The monster bellowed in fury, its wound seeping a strange, glowing liquid that burned with unnatural intensity. Irfan didn't have time to think—he was too focused on surviving the assault.

The fight was chaotic, the monster lashing out with a ferocity that kept the team on edge. Irfan fought with everything he had, but the more he engaged, the stronger the sense of familiarity became. The way the creature recoiled when injured, the almost human-like flashes in its movements—it was unsettling.

"This can't be..." Irfan muttered under his breath, the realization clawing at the edges of his mind. *"It's... like someone I know."*

The monster roared again, swiping at a support beam. The resulting collapse sent debris flying in all directions, forcing the team to scatter. When the dust settled, the monster was gone, its hulking form vanished.

"Irfan!" Priya called urgently, her voice echoing through the smoke-filled room. *"Over here!"*

Irfan turned, his heart sinking as he saw what Priya had found. Lying amidst the rubble, half-buried but unmistakably alive, was Arjun. His body was battered, his clothes torn, and blood pooled beneath him. Irfan's gaze locked on the deep gash across Arjun's shoulder—the exact place where he had wounded the monster just moments before. The wound was jagged, glowing faintly, and the blood that seeped from it hissed on the ground in the same way the monster's had.

Irfan's mind raced as the pieces fell into place.

The monster's movements. The strange, unexplainable changes Arjun had been experiencing.

The absence during the attacks. It all pointed to one terrifying possibility.

Arjun stirred as Irfan crouched beside him, his voice soft but firm. *"Arjun... what happened here?"*

Arjun groaned, his eyes fluttering open. *"I... don't remember,"* he mumbled, his voice weak. *"There was... fire. Then nothing."*

Irfan clenched his jaw, torn between his loyalty to his friend and the evidence mounting against him. *"Priya, scan the area. Collect anything that might give us answers."*

Priya nodded, pulling out her equipment and beginning a detailed sweep of the site. Nearby, Rohit carefully collected a vial of the monster's blood from where it had fallen, the faintly glowing liquid pulsing with an unnatural energy.

As the team worked, Irfan's gaze remained fixed on Arjun. Finally, he made the call. *"Restrain him,"* he said, his voice heavy.

"What?" Priya asked, looking up sharply.

"I don't want to believe it either," Irfan admitted, his tone bitter. *"But until we figure out what's going on, we can't take any chances. The changes we've seen in him... it matches what I just fought."*

Reluctantly, the team followed his order. Arjun didn't resist as they secured him, his head hung low in exhaustion and confusion. His breathing was shallow, his eyes distant, and the wound on his shoulder still burned with an unsettling energy.

CHAPTER FOURTEEN

BOUND BY FIRE

Back at the IRF base, Arjun was placed in a containment cell within the medical wing, his restraints monitored closely. The sterile walls and harsh lighting only added to the tension in the air as Irfan stood outside, staring through the reinforced glass. His mind raced, replaying the fight with the monster at Victor's house—the way it moved, the raw power it exuded, and the strange sense of familiarity that unsettled him to his core.

Inside the cell, Arjun sat on the cot, his head in his hands. His voice was quiet, almost pleading. *"I... I went there to check something. I thought I could find answers about what's been happening. Victor's research seemed connected, so I wanted to see if there was anything left behind."*

Irfan raised an eyebrow, skepticism etched across his face. *"And then what? The place was on fire, Arjun. It wasn't some research field trip."*

Arjun shook his head, frustration breaking through his usual calm. *"I don't know what happened after that. There was an explosion, and then... nothing. I blacked out. The next thing I remember, I woke up, and you were there."*

Irfan's gaze lingered on Arjun, searching for any hint of deception. But all he saw was genuine confusion—and fear. Still, the fight at Victor's home haunted him. The way the monster moved, the injury, the strange energy it exuded—it felt too familiar. And yet, it couldn't be Arjun... could it?

"Until we figure this out, you're staying here," Irfan said finally, his tone clipped. *"For your safety. And ours."*

Arjun leaned forward, desperation edging into his voice. *"Irfan, I'm telling you the truth. I didn't do this. Whatever that thing was—it wasn't me. You have to believe me."*

Irfan flinched slightly at Arjun's words but didn't reply. His jaw tightened, and his hands clenched into fists at his sides. *"I don't know what to believe right now, Arjun,"* he admitted, his voice softer but still strained.

Before Arjun could respond, the door to the observation room slid open, and Priya entered, holding the samples she and Rohit had collected. She avoided Arjun's gaze as she addressed Irfan. *"I'll start analyzing the blood and whatever else we found at the scene,"* she said. *"If there's something connecting him to the monster, we'll find it."*

Irfan nodded, though his jaw tightened at her words. He didn't want to believe it. He didn't want to think his best friend could be responsible for the destruction they'd witnessed. But the evidence—or the lack of answers—was painting a troubling picture.

As Priya left to begin her analysis, Arjun spoke again, his voice filled with frustration and pain. *"Irfan, you've known me for years. You know I wouldn't hurt anyone. I wouldn't—"*

"I know," Irfan interrupted sharply, his voice cracking slightly. He turned away, unable to meet Arjun's eyes. *"I know who you've been, Arjun. But I don't know what's happening to you now. And until we figure it out..."* He trailed off, the weight of his emotions hanging heavy in the air.

Arjun leaned back, his hands gripping the edge of the cot. *"Please, just listen—"*

"I can't," Irfan cut him off, his voice strained. He took a deep breath, his hand rubbing the back of his neck as if trying to calm himself. *"Not right now."*

Arjun opened his mouth to say more but stopped when he saw the look in Irfan's eyes—conflicted, tormented. Irfan turned back toward the glass, staring at Arjun as though searching for answers he wasn't ready to hear.

"I need some air," Irfan muttered finally, his voice barely audible. He stepped out of the room, leaving Arjun alone in the silence of the containment cell.

Outside, Irfan leaned against the cold metal wall, closing his eyes as the weight of the situation pressed down on him. His mind replayed every moment of the fight at Victor's house—the way the monster moved, its energy, and that fleeting sense of familiarity. It felt like Arjun, but it couldn't be.

"Irfan," Priya's voice cut through his thoughts. She was standing in the hallway, her expression tense. *"I'll let you know as soon as I have the results from the samples."*

He nodded absently, running a hand through his hair. *"Thanks."*

Priya hesitated before speaking again. *"You don't think it's him, do you?"*

Irfan's eyes flicked toward the observation room, where Arjun sat, his silhouette visible through the glass. *"I don't want to,"* he said quietly. *"But what if it is?"*

Priya didn't reply, her silence saying more than words could. She turned and walked away, leaving Irfan alone with his thoughts.

For now, all Irfan could do was wait—and hope the truth wasn't what he feared. But deep down, a nagging doubt whispered that everything was about to change.

CHAPTER FIFTEEN

A Promise in the Dark

The dim lights of the IRF base flickered as Irfan leaned against the wall outside the observation room, his eyes fixed on Arjun's containment cell. The tension in his chest was unbearable, the weight of uncertainty pressing down on him. He hadn't said much to anyone, but deep down, a nagging fear gnawed at him.

He reached for his phone, his fingers shaking as he dialed Taara's number. The call rang once... twice... then she picked up.

"Irfan?" Taara's voice was soft, but there was an immediate edge of panic to it. *"Did you find Arjun? Is he okay?"*

Irfan hesitated, his heart sinking. He didn't want to do this over the phone, but there was no other choice. *"Yeah, we found him."* His voice faltered slightly as he tried to keep it together. *"He's at the base. We... we've got him contained for now."*

"Contained?" Taara's voice went tight, almost desperate. *"What's going on, Irfan? What do you mean, 'contained'? Why is he there? What happened to him?"*

Irfan took a deep breath, struggling to steady his nerves. He couldn't tell her everything—not yet. Not when he didn't have the answers himself. *"Taara, I can't explain it all right now. I just need you to stay calm. He's not in danger, but we need to figure out what's going on with him."*

Taara's voice cracked, and he could hear her breath catch. *"I don't understand, Irfan. Is he okay? Is he... is he—did he do something? Is he responsible for this?"* She was breathing faster now, and Irfan felt the weight of her worry pressing against him.

"I don't know. I don't know what's happening to him," Irfan admitted, his voice thick with frustration. *"But something's changed, and we need answers. Just—just stay calm. Please."*

The silence on the other end of the line was deafening, and Irfan could practically feel her heart racing. *"I—I don't care what's happened to him, Irfan. You have to bring him back. He's not like this. I know he's not."*

"I know, Taara," Irfan said softly, his voice strained. *"I know who he is. But something's not right. I'm trying to get to the bottom of it, I swear."*

Taara's voice trembled. *"Please, tell me it's a mistake. Tell me you've got it wrong."*

"I wish I could. I wish I had answers, Taara," Irfan said, his throat tightening with guilt. *"But right now, I don't have anything solid. I just—just need you to stay safe. Please don't do anything."*

"I can't just sit here, Irfan," she whispered, her voice breaking. *"He's my everything. Please... just tell him I'm here. I'll wait for him."*

Irfan closed his eyes, fighting the wave of emotion that threatened to break through. *"I'll tell him, Taara. I promise. Just... stay calm. I'll figure this out."*

There was a long pause before Taara spoke again, her voice barely audible. *"Please be careful, Irfan. I'm trusting you with him."*

"I will," Irfan replied, his voice shaking slightly.

He hung up, staring at the phone for a moment, her words echoing in his mind. *"I'm trusting you with him."*

For the first time, Irfan wasn't sure if he could keep that promise.

CHAPTER SIXTEEN

CHAOS AT THE CORE

The IRF base was cloaked in uneasy silence when the attack came, shattering the calm. The alarms blared, painting the halls in a frantic, blood-red hue as soldiers scrambled into defensive positions. The ground trembled under the force of an explosion that tore through the outer perimeter.

"Defensive positions now!" Irfan barked, his voice rising above the chaos as he rallied the team. But something about the attack felt deeply wrong. The creature they had fought at Victor's house had been formidable, but this—this felt like an unstoppable force.

Irfan, Priya, and Rohit hurried through the base's main corridor, weapons ready, their hearts pounding in unison with the echo of destruction that shook the walls around them.

"What's the situation?" Priya shouted as they reached the control room.

"It's massive," one of the guards responded, his face pale. *"It's already breached the second layer of defenses. It's heading for the core."*

Irfan's fists clenched as he turned to Priya. *"Get whatever intel you can on this thing. Rohit, secure the research lab. We can't afford to lose the samples."*

Priya nodded, but her face betrayed her fear. *"We have no idea what we're dealing with. It could be—"*

Her words were drowned out by the deafening roar of the monster as it appeared on the surveillance screen. Hulking and monstrous, it moved like a living nightmare, its glowing red eyes scanning the destruction with ruthless intent. Its massive form smashed through walls, the jagged edges of its claws cutting through reinforced steel like paper.

"Is it the same one from Victor's house?" Priya asked, her voice trembling.

Irfan stared at the screen, his mind racing. The creature was familiar, but it wasn't exactly the same. There was something more deliberate, more ferocious about this one. *"I don't know. But we need to stop it before it takes the whole base down."*

The team sprinted toward the lower levels, where the monster had broken through. As they reached the scene, the sight stopped them in their tracks. The creature towered over the ruins of a collapsed wall, its grotesque, twisted form illuminated by the flickering emergency lights.

"Spread out!" Irfan ordered, his voice sharp with urgency. *"We need to contain it!"*

The team moved quickly, circling the beast, but their attacks barely slowed it. The monster swung its massive arms, sending soldiers flying across the room.

"Irfan, this isn't working!" Rohit shouted, firing off a burst of rounds that barely made a dent in the creature's thick hide.

"It's not about stopping it," Irfan growled. *"It's about surviving until we figure out how!"*

As the team fought desperately, something in Irfan's gut twisted. The way the monster moved—the rage in its attacks—it felt disturbingly familiar, like an echo of something he couldn't quite place.

"Priya, any scans on this thing?" Irfan called out as he dodged a massive claw.

"I'm working on it!" Priya shouted back, frantically analyzing the data streaming into her tablet.

But before she could respond, a new presence entered the fray.

In the sterile confines of the IRF base's medical wing, Arjun stirred awake. His head pounded with fragments of memories—images flashing in and out—none of them clear. The hum of the machines, the faint click of the overhead lights, the oppressive air of the containment cell—it all felt suffocating. He tried to sit up, only to be met with the biting sensation of the restraints that held him in place.

His breath quickened as he struggled to gather his thoughts. *"What's happening...?"* Arjun muttered, his voice hoarse, barely above a whisper. His mind was clouded with confusion and fear. The last thing he remembered was Victor's house—the explosion, the monster, the fire—and then nothing. He is trying to put everything together.

Then it came, a pulse of energy that surged through his veins like wildfire, far more intense than anything he had felt before. It wasn't just physical—it was instinctual, primal, as if something deep within him was waking up. The Phoenix's influence was there, its power coursing through him, urging him toward the chaos unfolding somewhere within the base.

The restraints groaned under the strain of his rising strength. Arjun gritted his teeth as the cuffs twisted and snapped, breaking free with a single, effortless motion.

"I need to stop this," he muttered, the urgency in his voice almost foreign to him. He didn't know what was happening or what he was about to face, but one thing was certain—he could no longer sit idly by.

Without another thought, Arjun sprinted down the hallway, moving faster and with more strength than he ever thought possible. The walls blurred past him as he zeroed in on the source of the destruction. As he ran, a feeling of something powerful deep inside him took hold—something dangerous, and yet strangely familiar. Arjun didn't stop, didn't slow down. He had to stop whatever was causing the chaos.

The sounds of destruction grew louder. Then, rounding a corner, he saw it—the monster. The creature that had once seemed so distant, so foreign, now stood before him. It was massive, grotesque, its body twisted and pulsing with unnatural energy. And there, in the midst of the destruction, Arjun's instincts kicked in.

Without hesitation, Arjun lunged toward the creature, his body moving with a speed and precision that seemed unnatural. The monster swung at him with massive arms, but Arjun was quick, dodging and landing blows of his own. The two of them fought, their movements blindingly fast, a blur of power and fury.

Irfan and the team watched in shock. They had expected Arjun to have transformed, to have become something monstrous, but as they observed, they realized something else. Arjun was fighting the creature with all his might, but he didn't look like the monster. He wasn't the creature they feared.

"I don't get it," Irfan muttered, confused. *"This isn't the Arjun we've known, but he's fighting like hell. He is not transformed?"*

Priya, standing by with her scanner, glanced at the readouts. *"He's not showing any signs of mutation. The readings are consistent with his normal vitals, just... enhanced strength."*

Still, the creature was too powerful. Arjun fought back with everything he had, but the monster was relentless. He managed to land a few blows, but nothing seemed to slow it down. In a split second, the creature lashed out, catching Arjun with a massive punch to the chest. The force sent Arjun crashing backward, his body hurtling through the air, slamming into the side of a building.

For a moment, everything went still. The dust settled. Arjun lay still for a second, his mind spinning. He felt like he was weightless, floating through the air. But then, just before he hit the building, something clicked. A strange sense of awareness flooded his senses—he could feel the energy around him, the air currents, the pull of gravity.

Before he could react, the ground rushed up to meet him, and everything went black.

CHAPTER SEVENTEEN

COLLISION OF TITANS

The monster roared, shaking the rubble-strewn ground as it towered over the wreckage of the IRF base. Its glowing red eyes burned with rage, scanning for its next target. Irfan and the team crouched behind a crumbled wall, their weapons trembling in their hands. The weight of the destruction around them was suffocating, and the team's focus was locked on the hulking figure advancing toward them.

"This is it," Irfan muttered, clutching his rifle. His eyes darted toward Priya, who stood frozen with her scanner in hand. *"Get ready. If that thing gets any closer, we're not going to—"*

Before he could finish, a guttural growl echoed through the air. A second creature emerged from the remains of a nearby building where Arjun fell, its massive form breaking through the smoke and dust. Its appearance was equally terrifying: jagged, chaotic, and pulsing with an unnatural energy. Unlike the Victor monster, this one's movements were erratic, almost feral, as though it was driven purely by rage and pain. A deep, glowing wound marred its shoulder, pulsing with an eerie light, the same strange energy that seemed to emanate from the monster's body, hissing as it bled onto the ground.

The IRF team froze, their eyes widening in shock. *"Another one?"* Rohit whispered, his voice barely audible over the chaos.

Irfan's breath caught, his mind racing to make sense of what he was seeing. His gaze fixed on the second creature, and a chill ran down his spine. *"It's... Arjun,"* he murmured, his voice heavy with disbelief. *"It has to be. He's changed again."*

Priya hesitated, lowering her scanner. *"Irfan, are you sure? That thing... it looks worse than before."*

Irfan gritted his teeth, anger and fear clashing in his expression. *"This is the monster I fought at Victor's house,"* he said firmly. *"I felt it then, and I'm feeling it now. The way it moves, the energy it radiates—it's the same. And look at the shoulder injury,"* he pointed toward the glowing wound on the creature's shoulder, pulsing with that unnatural light. *"It's identical to what I saw back there. Arjun's lost control. He's completely turned."*

The team silently agreed, their fear confirming what seemed obvious. The changes Arjun had described—the strength, the energy—they now saw them reflected in the twisted, monstrous form of the second creature. There could be no other explanation.

"I knew it," Irfan muttered, his voice tightening with frustration. *"The signs were there—the changes, the power... I should've stopped him sooner."*

Priya frowned, her gaze darting between the two creatures. *"But what about the Big monster? If Arjun's this one... then what's—"*

"We'll deal with that later," Irfan interrupted, his tone sharp. His

eyes stayed locked on the second creature. *"Right now, we have to stop them both before they destroy everything."*

The two monsters—the first massive creature and the second beast—finally turned their attention to one another. A deep, guttural snarl erupted from the second creature as it lunged forward, its massive claws slicing through the air. *"Victor!"* the creature howled, its voice raw with fury. The name echoed, reverberating with pain and rage.

The IRF team froze, their eyes widening in shock as the creature bellowed the name. *"Victor?"* Priya whispered, her voice filled with disbelief. The connection was undeniable, and the realization hit them hard. The creature wasn't just attacking—it was calling out to someone. Someone who was deeply tied to this chaos.

Victor's monster roared in response, meeting the charge head-on. But the team's focus had already shifted, their thoughts racing to piece together the significance of the shout.

"This isn't random," Irfan muttered, his eyes narrowing. *"There's a deeper connection here. But what does it mean?"*

Rohit, who had been quietly analyzing the situation, suddenly spoke up. *"Wait... Victor?"* He paused, a thought clearly forming in his mind. *"Victor... That name... I've seen it before."*

"What are you talking about?" Irfan asked, his attention shifting to Rohit.

Rohit quickly pulled out his tablet and began typing furiously. *"Victor Kane. He was a scientist at IRF before... before he disappeared. I remember reading his files. He was involved in advanced research—genetics, mutation... and something about immortality. But all the records on him suddenly went dark. There's nothing recent. He was experimenting with biological enhancements, and from what I've gathered... he disappeared, leaving behind a trail of wrecked projects."*

Priya frowned, trying to piece things together. *"So... Victor was here? He was part of the IRF?"*

Rohit nodded slowly, his brow furrowed. *"Yes, and based on what we've seen, it looks like he was researching far beyond what anyone should. We never had concrete evidence, but his work was dangerous. He could have been looking for something... or someone."* Rohit glanced at the battle unfolding before them. *"And now we know that whatever he was working on... it's still here. This isn't just an attack. This is personal. This creature—this monster—it's connected to him."*

Priya's expression shifted as something clicked in her mind. *"I remember now. Some of the wrecked projects we found... there was a whole section on genetic manipulation, experimental viruses, and the creation of hybrids. They were developing advanced regenerative treatments and alterations to human biology at the cellular level. But most of those experiments were abandoned."*

Irfan's attention snapped to Priya. *"So, Victor was trying to create something... something beyond human?"*

Priya nodded grimly. *"Exactly. He was experimenting with life—changing it, enhancing it. It's not just about power or survival for him. If these creatures are part of his research, it's clear he's been trying to perfect something beyond our understanding."*

Irfan clenched his fists. *"Then the real question is... what is Victor searching for? What does he want with all of this?"* His voice was thick with frustration. *"We need answers, and fast. If we don't stop him, if we don't figure out what he's after, this could spiral out of control."*

The team fell silent, each member processing the disturbing implications of Rohit's and Priya's revelations. The weight of the situation pressed down on them as they realized the monster before them wasn't just an attack—it was part of something much bigger, something far more dangerous than they had imagined.

The collision was deafening. The force of their impact sent shockwaves rippling through the ground, toppling what remained of the nearby structures. Victor's immense bulk gave him the advantage in brute strength, but the second monster's erratic movements made it unpredictable. It struck with a frenzy, claws raking across Victor's glowing torso, leaving jagged scorch marks.

Irfan and the team watched in stunned silence, their weapons forgotten for the moment as the battle unfolded before them.

"This... this doesn't make sense," Priya whispered, her hands trembling as she held her scanner. *"Why would it—why would he—fight the Victor monster?"*

"Maybe it's instinct," Rohit suggested, his voice shaky. *"A fight for dominance or... survival?"*

Irfan remained silent, his jaw clenched. His heart told him that something wasn't adding up, but the evidence before his eyes was undeniable—or so he thought.

The battle intensified. The second monster's attacks were relentless, its claws striking Victor with calculated fury, as though it harbored a personal grudge. The ferocity of the fight felt primal, driven by something deeper than mere aggression. Victor, with his overwhelming size and raw power, eventually gained the upper hand. With a thunderous blow, he struck the second monster square in the chest, sending it skidding across the ground. The impact left deep trenches in the dirt as the creature's massive body finally came to a halt, motionless.

TRIAD OF FURY

The second monster lay there, seemingly unconscious, its massive frame heaving faintly with shallow breaths. For a moment, the battlefield grew eerily quiet, the only sound the crackling of distant flames and the low, guttural growls emanating from Victor as he turned his glowing red eyes toward the IRF team.

"It's down..." Rohit whispered, his voice trembling with a mix of relief and dread.

"Don't count on it," Irfan muttered, his grip tightening on his rifle. *"We're not out of this yet."*

Victor roared, shaking the ground with the force of his anger, and began to lumber toward the team. The IRF members scrambled to retreat, their weapons raised but their faces betraying their fear.

"We can't stop that thing," Priya said, her voice cracking. *"If it gets any closer—"*

Before she could finish, a sudden burst of heat warped the air. A fiery explosion of energy erupted, throwing dust and debris into the air. From the chaos emerged a blur—a figure encased in blazing light, cutting through the smoke like a comet.

Arjun.

He soared through the sky, flames trailing behind him as the air around him rippled with intense heat. His body glowed like the heart of a furnace, the Phoenix's influence coursing through him, reshaping him. His eyes burned with an ethereal light as he descended toward Victor, the sheer force of his power sending shockwaves through the ground.

In one fluid motion, Arjun's fist, engulfed in searing flame, collided with Victor's massive form. The impact was cataclysmic, the force of the blow cracking the earth beneath them and sending shockwaves that reverberated for miles. The ground trembled as Victor staggered back, roaring in pain, his towering frame nearly knocked off balance.

The moment hung in the air like a charged silence. Flames erupted around Arjun, his body glowing with a fierce, otherworldly light as he hovered, fully realizing his power for the first time. The heat was unbearable, and the sheer intensity of his presence was enough to make the IRF team step back in awe and terror.

The IRF team froze in disbelief. Irfan's rifle lowered slightly as he watched Arjun, his body engulfed in flames, battling Victor with a renewed intensity. For the first time, doubt crept into Irfan's mind—was Arjun really the monster they feared? But as Victor swung at Arjun with massive, clawed hands, the answer became clear: Arjun was fighting to protect them.

The fight between Victor and Arjun escalated, their blows creating shockwaves that toppled nearby debris. Flames erupted from Arjun's fists as he struck Victor with precision, countering the brute force of the larger monster. But Victor, enraged by the resistance, lunged at Arjun, catching him midair and slamming him into the ground.

Arjun groaned in pain, but the flames around him reignited, his body healing at an accelerated rate. He launched himself back into the air, his feet never touching the ground as he hovered, flames surrounding him like a storm. With a fiery punch, he struck Victor again, sending the massive creature reeling backward. The impact caused the ground to tremble beneath them as Arjun pressed his advantage, striking with precision and force.

Victor, battered and enraged, swung a massive claw at Arjun, but he dodged the strike with ease, his speed unmatched. Arjun's attacks were relentless, each blow landing with the force of an inferno. With one final, earth-shattering punch, he slammed Victor into the ground, creating a massive crater beneath the monster. Victor let out a roar of agony before falling still, his body twitching only once before it lay motionless.

For a moment, the battlefield fell silent as Arjun hovered above the destruction, flames still crackling around him. His chest heaved with effort, but he remained focused, his mind racing as he scanned the scene. Before he could process what had just happened, a deep, guttural roar broke the silence.

As the battle raged on, the IRF team watched, their eyes glued to the unfolding chaos.

"This doesn't make sense," Priya muttered, her hands gripping her scanner tightly. **"Arjun's not the monster. So who the hell is the**

second one?"

Priya's eyes flickered to her scanner as she processed and checked the blood sample data. Her breath caught, and her voice trembled. She whispered, her heart racing. *"It is Ashwath."*

Irfan's gaze snapped to her, disbelief flashing across his face. "Ashwath?" he echoed, his voice thick with shock. *"The second monster—it's Ashwath?"*

Priya nodded, her face pale. *"The blood from Victor's house wasn't Arjun's. It was Ashwath's."*

Irfan stood frozen, trying to digest the impossible reality unfolding before them. The monster they'd been fighting wasn't the person they thought it was—and the battle was far from over.

Irfan's mind reeled as the pieces clicked into place. The anger, the volatility, the disappearance—it all made sense now. He felt a wave of relief wash over him as he realized Arjun wasn't the monster he had fought before. But his relief was short-lived as the second monster—Ashwath—began to stir.

Ashwath's monstrous form rose from where it had fallen, his body pulsating with an eerie energy. His eyes burned with fury, glowing a deep, hellish red. He let out a guttural roar, filled with rage and anguish, and without hesitation, charged at Arjun. The ground trembled with each step as the two collided once again.

Arjun, caught off guard, launched himself into the air, dodging a savage swipe from Ashwath. His flames flared, illuminating the chaos around him, as he maneuvered quickly. He landed a powerful punch to Ashwath's chest, sending the creature staggering backward. Ashwath growled in pain, but the fiery impact didn't stop him; instead, it seemed to fuel his fury.

The battle became a chaotic three-way fight. Ashwath's strikes were wild, driven by a primal need for vengeance. His attacks were brutal, fueled by raw emotion, and he fought with a savagery that was hard to contain. Arjun fought back with calculated precision, each blow a fiery testament to his growing power. His fists, ablaze with energy, connected with Ashwath's monstrous form with devastating force.

The ground beneath them cracked and splintered as they exchanged blows. Arjun ducked and weaved, his movements fluid despite the chaos, and finally landed a crushing punch to Ashwath's side. The force of the blow sent the creature sprawling, its body slamming into the dirt and leaving a deep trench behind.

As the chaos unfolded, the IRF team tried to make sense of the situation.

"Irfan, we need to get to Arjun," Priya shouted, her voice filled with urgency. *"He has to know the truth."*

Irfan's eyes flickered toward Arjun, still circling above the fight. *"How do we get to him?"* he asked, frustration clear in his voice.

Without hesitation, Priya pulled out a flare gun and aimed it at the sky. Her hands were trembling as she fired it, the bright trail cutting through the smoke-filled air. The flare soared toward Arjun, catching his attention as he glanced down.

Arjun, his fiery aura glowing brighter, swooped down toward the team. He hovered just above them, flames illuminating the scene in a ghostly light.

Irfan's voice broke through the roar of the battle. *"Arjun!"* he called, urgency in his tone. *"The second monster—it's Ashwath!"*

Arjun hovered mid-air, his eyes narrowing as he focused on the second beast, still lying motionless from their previous clash. His heart skipped a beat as he saw the twisted form of his old comrade—Ashwath, now a monstrous version of the man he once knew. The flames around Arjun flickered as he processed the realization. This battle wasn't just about survival anymore—it was a fight to save what remained of his humanity.

With a sharp breath, Arjun steadied himself and dove back into the fray. The sky above the battlefield burned with his fiery intensity.

Arjun took to the skies, his body a blazing comet as he circled above the chaos. Flames illuminated the ruined base below, casting long, eerie shadows across the wreckage. He watched as Ashwath relentlessly clawed and bit at Victor, his monstrous form nearly unrecognizable from the man Arjun once called a friend.

"Ashwath, stop!" Arjun shouted, his voice cutting through the cacophony. But Ashwath's rage blinded him. The creature's focus remained solely on Victor, its fury all-consuming.

Victor seized an opening, swinging his massive arm with terrifying force. He slammed Ashwath into the ground once again, the impact sending a shockwave that rattled the ground beneath them. But Ashwath, driven by a primal need for vengeance, didn't relent. He rose almost immediately and charged back at Victor with renewed vigor.

Realizing the danger to both his friend and the team, Arjun dove into the battle. His fiery aura erupted around him, flames swirling as he launched a searing blast straight at Victor, forcing the massive creature to stagger back.

The battlefield was chaos incarnate—fire, rage, and destruction colliding in a maelstrom of power. Irfan and the team watched from a safe distance, their disbelief giving way to determination.

"We need to help Arjun," Irfan said, his voice steady, eyes locked on the fight.

"But what about Ashwath?" Rohit asked, fear lacing his words.

Irfan hesitated, his gaze fixed on the monstrous figure battling Victor. **"We'll deal with that when the time comes. Right now, we focus on surviving."**

As the fight raged on, Arjun, Ashwath, and Victor clashed in a deadly dance of power and fury. Each blow shook the earth, and each roar echoed with the weight of their struggle. In the heart of the chaos, the lines between friend and foe blurred, but one thing was clear—this was a battle that would change everything.

FALLING INTO THE FIRE

The battleground was chaos. Dust and debris choked the air, the sound of crashing metal and the roar of battle filling the once-quiet IRF base. Ashwath, in his monstrous form, clashed violently with Victor, the two titans locked in a battle of destruction. Arjun, battered and bruised, hovered nearby, ready to jump in.

Victor, with his overwhelming size and strength, had the upper hand for a time. But Ashwath, driven by rage, relentlessly fought back. The two were locked in a furious exchange, each blow sending shockwaves through the air. Arjun, his fiery presence illuminating the chaos around him, watched the destruction unfold.

This has to stop, Arjun thought. This can't continue.

Realizing that the battle was spiraling out of control, Arjun knew it was time to intervene. But not in the way he had before. This time, he had to separate Ashwath from the fight and try to bring his friend back to his senses. He could feel the heat of his flames surging inside him, but he kept his focus sharp.

I can't let this go on.

Arjun dove toward Ashwath, pushing the battle between Victor and the monstrous version of his friend to the side. He flew low, streaking through the air with a burst of speed, and tackled Ashwath, trying to knock him out of the fray. The collision sent both creatures tumbling to the ground, the impact shaking the earth beneath them.

Ashwath roared in fury, swiping at Arjun, his massive claws leaving scorch marks across the ground. But Arjun was determined to stop this. He dove into the fight, his body ablaze with fiery energy, and pulled Ashwath back with all his strength, forcing the creature to turn toward him.

"Ashwath!" Arjun shouted, his voice cutting through the cacophony of battle. *"You're still in there! Fight this! You can control it!"*

Ashwath's monstrous form paused, his body trembling as if torn between the rage that consumed him and the flickers of humanity that Arjun was desperately trying to reach. The heat around Arjun intensified, and he could feel his power surging, but he focused on keeping his connection to Ashwath strong, using his words to break through the chaos.

"I know you're still in there," Arjun said, his voice softer now, his hand reaching out toward his friend. *"This isn't you. You're not a monster. You can still fight this!"*

For a moment, Ashwath hesitated. His glowing red eyes flickered, the fury in them dimming just slightly. He growled, shaking his massive head as if trying to clear his mind.

Arjun pressed on, his voice firm, yet gentle. *"Please, Ashwath, stop.*

This doesn't have to be the end. You're not lost."

The battle around them seemed to slow, the noise muffled as Arjun's words began to take hold. Ashwath's breathing steadied, though his monstrous form still trembled with barely-contained anger.

Victor, sensing an opportunity, let out a ferocious roar and lunged at Arjun, claws outstretched. But just as Victor reached them, Ashwath reacted with sudden clarity. He stepped forward, his monstrous claws raised, not in anger but in protection.

"No!" Ashwath roared, his voice thick with emotion. ***"This ends now!"***

With one powerful swing, Ashwath intercepted Victor's strike, blocking it with his massive body. The impact shook the ground, but Ashwath stood firm, a newfound resolve in his eyes.

Arjun, seeing his friend regain control, surged forward, unleashing a torrent of flames that forced Victor to stagger back. The combined strength of Arjun and Ashwath created a powerful synergy, their efforts working in unison to push Victor back.

Together, they fought as a team. Arjun's flames blazed brightly, each strike delivering precise blows to Victor's towering form. Ashwath, still monstrous but now with the clarity of purpose, used his brute strength to block Victor's attacks and retaliate with powerful strikes. The two creatures, once enemies, now fought together—fueled by a shared resolve to stop the destruction.

"Ashwath, together!" Arjun shouted, his voice filled with urgency.

With a final, earth-shattering punch, Ashwath tackled Victor to the ground, while Arjun soared into the air. Arjun, fueled by his power and the strength of his newfound alliance with Ashwath, launched one last, massive wave of fire toward Victor, engulfing the monstrous creature in a storm of flames.

Victor screamed, thrashing in the flames, but it was no use. The combined might of Arjun and Ashwath overwhelmed him, and soon, the ground beneath them grew still. The battle was over. Victor, once the unstoppable force of destruction, lay motionless.

For a moment, silence descended over the battlefield, the smoke and fire still lingering in the air. Then, through the crackling flames, Victor's voice—raspy and filled with rage—escaped his lips ending with a chilling sound.

"Hhh...Aaan..."

As the finality of Victor's defeat settled over the battlefield, the IRF team stood in stunned silence, breathing heavily, the air thick with smoke and the lingering heat. It seemed like the battle was finally over, and relief washed over them.

Rohit, still wide-eyed, glanced around, trying to shake the unease lingering in his chest. *"Did... did Victor say something?"* he asked, his voice tentative, filled with curiosity.

Before anyone could respond, the ground beneath them trembled, and distant explosions echoed through the air. The team snapped their attention back to the aftermath of the battle, the urgency returning.

"Focus, Rohit," Irfan said sharply, his voice tight as he looked

toward the wreckage. ***"We've got more to worry about right now."***

Rohit's question hung in the air, unanswered, as the team scrambled to assess the damage.

Ashwath, breathing heavily, turned to face Arjun. His monstrous form still loomed, but his eyes, filled with remorse, now held the humanity they had lost for so long.

"I'm sorry, Arjun," Ashwath said quietly, his voice trembling with regret. ***"I didn't know what I was becoming."***

Arjun placed a steadying hand on Ashwath's massive shoulder, his expression softening. ***"You're not alone,"*** he said, his voice firm with understanding. ***"We'll fix this. Together."***

As the dust began to settle, Irfan and the team approached cautiously, their weapons still drawn but their expressions shifting from suspicion to tentative trust. The sight of Ashwath and Arjun, no longer enemies but allies, marked a pivotal moment in their struggle.

The battle for the IRF base was over, but questions about the future of Arjun and Ashwath loomed large.

What would become of them?

For now, the fight had ended, but the uncertainty of what came next lingered.

CHAPTER TWENTY

WHISPERS OF THE PHOENIX

The first rays of dawn filtered through the cracks in the IRF base, casting a soft light over the aftermath of the battle. The air was heavy with an uneasy calm, as though the base itself was holding its breath.

Ashwath was starting the hard road to redemption.

Arjun, his body still sore from the fight, walked into the briefing room where Rohit sat hunched over a console. The glow of the screens reflected in his glasses as he meticulously cataloged damage reports from the previous night.

Arjun placed a charred but intact communication device and a damaged CCTV module on the table in front of him.

"Can you recover anything from these?" Arjun asked, his voice steady but laced with urgency.

Rohit picked up the CCTV, inspecting its condition. **"It's pretty banged up, but I'll see what I can do,"** he replied, raising an eyebrow.

"Where did you get these?"

Arjun hesitated for a moment, weighing his words. *"From Kiltan Island,"* he finally said. *"The lab near the radiation machine. I found them buried in the debris."*

Irfan, who had just entered the room, overheard the exchange. His eyes narrowed as he stepped closer. *"Wait, you went back to Kiltan Island?"*

Arjun turned to face him, meeting his gaze. *"Yes,"* he said simply.

"You went back to Kiltan Island, dug through the wreckage, and found these," Irfan said, his voice growing sharper with each word. *"And you decided to keep this little field trip to yourself? Why didn't you tell me about the CCTV and the communication device? Why keep it secret?"*

Arjun sighed, rubbing the back of his neck. His posture was calm, but there was a note of defiance in his voice. *"I didn't want to tell anyone till I found the answers,"* he said bluntly.

Irfan clenched his jaw, a mix of frustration and guilt flashing across his face. He knew Arjun was right, but admitting it felt like swallowing shards of glass. *"You should've told me, at least when you were in Medical prison."*

Arjun's expression softened slightly. *"And what would you have said if I told you back then? You weren't ready to listen, Irfan. Not after everything that happened."*

Irfan's eyes darkened at the mention of Victor's house. He crossed his arms and leaned slightly closer. *"Okay, explain something to me,*

Arjun," he said slowly. *"How did we find you there—right after the monster disappeared?"*

Arjun hesitated, his gaze dropping to the table before he spoke. *"When I found these on the island, I was searching the place to see if I could get some lead. Then I got a receipt for a chemical, something that mentioned Victor's address. It seemed linked to the lab's work... I thought it might lead me to more answers about what's been happening—about the radiation, the phoenix, everything. So I went to Victor's house to investigate."*

Irfan's jaw tightened. *"And?"*

"I heard someone breaking in," Arjun continued, his voice steady but heavy with emotion. *"It wasn't you—I would've recognized your approach. So I panicked. I went to the basement to hide."* He looked up, meeting Irfan's gaze. *"That's all I remember until I woke up and saw you standing in front of me."*

Irfan rubbed the back of his neck, conceding the point with a grudging nod. *"Fine. But next time, don't keep this stuff to yourself. We're supposed to be in this together."*

Arjun's lips twitched into a faint smirk. *"You mean even when you're a stubborn idiot?"*

Irfan chuckled despite himself, the tension between them easing slightly. *"Don't push your luck."*

As the two shared a rare moment of levity, Rohit looked up from his console, his eyes wide with excitement. *"Hey, I'm already getting something from the CCTV,"* he announced. *"The communication device might take a while to decrypt, but... it's definitely worth the wait."*

Both Arjun and Irfan turned their attention to the screens, their brief moment of calm replaced by a renewed sense of urgency.

"What's on it?" Arjun asked, his voice tight with anticipation.

Rohit shook his head. *"Not sure yet, but there's definitely something here. Give me some time to clean up the footage and piece it together."*

Arjun nodded, a mix of relief and tension settling over him. Whatever secrets these devices held, they were one step closer to understanding the chaos they had been thrust into. And for the first time in days, Arjun felt like he was finally moving toward the answers he had been searching for.

CHAPTER TWENTY-ONE

FROM ASHES, THE TRUTH

The IRF team assembled in the dimly lit briefing room, the weight of recent events palpable in the air. Rohit stood by the console, his face tense but focused. The faint hum of the monitor was the only sound as everyone settled into their seats, the gravity of the meeting reflected in their silence.

"I managed to recover part of the footage," Rohit began, his voice steady but laced with anticipation. *"It's not much—it's from just before the lab collapsed on Kiltan Island. But it might explain... everything."*

All eyes turned to the screen as Rohit pressed play. The shaky, grainy footage showed the interior of the crumbled lab. The radiation machine was visible in the background, its ominous hum still present. Then, as the radiation burst, the Phoenix appeared—a glowing figure that streaked across the frame like a comet.

The room was bathed in flickering light as the Phoenix moved between Arjun and the radiation. Its fiery wings flared brilliantly, enveloping Arjun in a shield of golden light. The footage froze on the moment the Phoenix shielded Arjun, leaving the room silent.

"That's it," Rohit said, pausing the footage and turning to face the team. *"That's why Arjun didn't transform. The Phoenix shielded him. Its energy... redirected the radiation. It protected him, altered the way it affected his body."*

Irfan leaned forward, his voice low and measured. *"And Ashwath?"*

Rohit hesitated before bringing up another file. *"Ashwath wasn't shielded. He was directly exposed to the radiation's full force. That's why he..."* He trailed off, unwilling to finish the sentence.

Ashwath, seated at the far corner of the room, stiffened. His face betrayed no emotion, but his clenched fists told another story.

"So that's it," Irfan muttered, more to himself than anyone else. *"It wasn't chance. It was the Phoenix."*

The room fell into a heavy silence. For a moment, no one spoke. The revelation left the team grappling with a mixture of relief and guilt. Arjun hadn't become the monster, but Ashwath had—through no fault of his own.

Ashwath finally broke the silence, his voice low and steady. *"It wasn't just the Phoenix. I chose to go into that lab. I made that decision to fix the circuit. And I've paid for it. But now... I'm choosing to fight back."*

Arjun nodded, his expression resolute. *"You're not doing it alone."*

The two exchanged a knowing look, their shared determination radiating through the room. The weight of their mistakes, their transformations, and their redemption bound them in a way that words couldn't.

CHAPTER TWENTY-TWO

SHADOWS EXPOSED

As the team began to rise from their seats, ready to leave the briefing room, Rohit's voice interrupted the silence once again. *"Oops, sorry—there's more,"* he said, his tone laced with urgency. *"I've recovered some of the pre-recorded messages, and I've also got one more CCTV clip."*

The team froze, the air thick with tension as they turned back toward Rohit. He gestured toward the console and hit a few keys, bringing the screen back to life.

Message 1 – Conversation with Victor on the Research:

Victor Kane's voice crackled through the speakers, filled with frustration and desperation. *"The Phoenix's regenerative abilities are unlike anything I've seen before. But… the serum isn't working. I need more time."*

Before Victor could continue, a sharp, cold voice interrupted. The distortion did little to mask its chilling authority.

"Victor, you don't have time. The Phoenix must be tested now. We need results—now. Failure is not an option. You will deliver, or I'll

find someone else who will."

Victor's voice quivered with fear. *"Understood. I'll make it work."*

The team exchanged uneasy glances, unsettled by the coldness of the voice. But it wasn't until the second message that the true identity of the voice was revealed.

Message 2 – Conversation with Mira:

Mira's voice came through next, calm but laced with urgency. *"Shaan, Victor's hesitating. He's afraid of what the Phoenix might do to him. We need to push him harder—emotionally. If he believes this is his last chance, he'll do it."*

The voice of Shaan, now unmistakable and chillingly clear, responded.

"Mira, you're the only one who can get through to him. Make him believe it's do or die. The Phoenix experiment must be completed. We need results now."

Rohit quickly typed something into the console, running the voice through the recognition software. His eyes widened as the results flashed across the screen.

"I ran the voice through the recognition software..." Rohit's voice shook with disbelief. *"It's confirmed. It's Shaan Raghav—the IRF Chief. He's been the one behind everything."*

As the final notes of Shaan's voice echoed in the room, a thick silence descended. The team was reeling from the bombshell dropped by Rohit's revelation. The gravity of their situation was beginning to sink in. But not everyone was fully convinced just yet.

"Wait," Irfan said, his voice sharp with disbelief. *"That voice—it could be anyone. The software could've gotten it wrong. I mean, it's not like it's a perfect match every time, right? Or maybe it's a recording from a bad sci-fi movie. It could be someone else."*

"Irfan's right," Priya chimed in, her brow furrowing. *"It's possible that it's just another voice, or... we could be missing something. We need more confirmation."*

Rohit, still looking at the data, was clearly frustrated. *"I'm sure of this,"* he insisted. *"I ran it through the recognition software. It's confirmed. It's Shaan."*

Then, his expression shifted slightly, and he hesitated for a moment before continuing. *"And... before Victor died, I swear I heard him make a sound. Something like 'hhh... aaaan.' What if... what if that was a reference to Shaan? What if he was looking for him in our base?"*

The room fell silent again, and the air seemed thicker with tension.

Irfan's eyes narrowed, still uncertain. *"You think Victor was calling for Shaan? That's a stretch. What's next, are we going to say he's got a secret love affair with him?"*

Priya shook her head slowly, a thought forming in her mind. *"But... what if he was?"*

Irfan raised an eyebrow. *"What love affair?"*

Priya's gaze sharpened. *"No, what if Victor was looking for Shaan here in our base? And now we're finding out he's behind all of this. If he was trying to get to him..."* She trailed off, the implications of her words hanging heavily in the air.

Rohit's fingers hovered over the console, his voice barely above a whisper. *"I don't know... It felt like more than just a random noise. It felt like he was naming someone. And if it was Shaan, then everything we thought we knew is wrong."*

The team exchanged uneasy glances, their doubts lingering in the air as they processed the new information. Even with Rohit's confirmation, there were still too many unanswered questions.

Rohit hit a few keys, and within seconds, a new video appeared on the screen. This one was brief—only a few seconds long—but the clarity of the footage was undeniable. It showed a dimly lit lab. Mira was standing by a lab table, her back to the camera. Shaan appeared from the shadows, walking toward her with purpose. They exchanged a few words, but their conversation was unclear.

However, the image of Shaan standing there, his presence undeniable, left no room for doubt. The team stood in stunned silence, processing the undeniable truth.

The tension in the room mounted, but it was broken when Ashwath, who had remained silent until now, stood up. His fists clenched, and his voice, filled with a mixture of fury and disbelief, broke the silence.

"The man who did this to us is right in front of us, and we can't just let him get away with it."

Arjun remained silent while staring at the screen.

Irfan looked at the screen, disbelief still etched on his face. *"We've been played, all along. Honestly, I should've seen this coming. First, he makes us fight for a decent paycheck, now he's making us fight for our lives. What's next, mandatory team-building on a deserted island?"*

The weight of the realization settled in. Shaan Raghav, their leader, the person they trusted, had orchestrated everything from the very beginning. And they had been pawns in his game.

Yet, amidst the betrayal and chaos, the phoenix endured. It had become a part of them—a symbol of rebirth and hope, but also a warning of the peril that came with unchecked power.

In the distance, the phoenix soared across the horizon, its fiery wings cutting through the twilight sky. It was a beacon, a reminder that their battle wasn't just for the world—it was for their own survival, their humanity, and the future they dared to reclaim.

The fire would rise again. But this time, they would wield its power. And they would decide its purpose.

The End?

The tension in the room was palpable. The team's minds were still reeling from the truth they'd just uncovered about Shaan Raghav. As the shock began to settle, a crackling sound suddenly filled the room—something stirring in the damaged communications system. The distorted voice echoed once more, and everyone went silent, knowing this was no mere glitch.

The cold, calculating voice of Shaan Raghav filled the room, unmistakable and chilling.

"Victor failed. The experiment's results are unstable, but we've learned enough. The Phoenix's power must be contained, and now we have the opportunity to use it."

Mira's voice followed, frustration and urgency creeping into her words.

"The Kryllis project is difficult, but we have no choice now. Combining the Phoenix's power could unlock something extraordinary."

Dr. Marcus's methodical tone joined in next.

"The combination of both creatures will give us an edge. The Phoenix's regenerative power, combined with the Kryllis' adaptability, will create something we can control—a force no one can defeat."

Shaan's voice returned, more chilling and authoritative than ever.

The team exchanged looks, disbelief mixing with a sense of urgency. Their leader, Shaan, had been orchestrating everything from the shadows, manipulating them all along. The threat they faced was more dangerous than they'd ever imagined.

As the final words of the communication faded, the tension reached its peak. And then, from the silence, a voice cut through—the voice of Arjun.

With determination in his eyes, Arjun stood and walked toward the console, his gaze fixed on the communication device. He picked up the mic, his hand steady despite the weight of the moment. His voice, clear and resolute, broke through the air.

"Arjun here. You'll be nothing but ash when we're done with you."

Fury unleashed.
The wings of destruction await.

Bonus Content: More About The Mystical Creatures

In Phoenix - Ashes and Fury, the world is teeming with mystical creatures—beings of immense power, mystery, and ancient origins. These creatures embody forces of nature, magic, and destiny, influencing the events and characters throughout the story. Here's a closer look at some of the mystical beings featured in the book, including the Phoenix, Kryllis, Serpent of Lumina, Thunder Wolf, Aether Drake, and the Basilisk.

Phoenix

The Phoenix is one of the most iconic creatures in mythology, but in Phoenix - Ashes and Fury, it is much more than just a symbol of rebirth. The Phoenix's wings, ablaze with an intense fire, shine like molten gold, lighting up the darkness around it. This mystical bird has the ability to rise from its own ashes, and with each rebirth, it grows stronger, its flame more powerful.

The Phoenix represents not only regeneration but the danger of unchecked power. As it burns and rises, it renews itself, but it also destroys everything in its path. This cycle of life, death, and rebirth is central to the story, symbolizing the characters' internal struggles and the transformations they must undergo to control their destinies. While the Phoenix brings hope and potential, its fire is both a gift and a curse—its power must be controlled, or it will consume all.

Kryllis

The Kryllis is one of the most enigmatic and powerful creatures in the world of Phoenix - Ashes and Fury. It exists between the tangible and the ethereal, shifting between forms that are both solid and spectral. Its glowing patterns shift and change constantly, as though its very body is made of light and shadow, fluctuating with an energy that's impossible to comprehend fully.

The Kryllis is a creature that commands the elements of light and darkness. It has the ability to manipulate both, creating illusions or cloaking itself from sight. Its red eyes glow with a deep, unsettling intensity, capable of seeing through the deepest veils of secrecy and revealing the truth. The Kryllis' true purpose remains shrouded in mystery, but it is clear that it is not merely a passive creature—it has the ability to influence events and people in ways no one fully understands.

Some believe that the Kryllis holds the key to unlocking unimaginable power, while others fear it is the harbinger of an inevitable destruction. It is a creature of contradictions—beautiful yet terrifying, powerful yet elusive—and its role in the world is far from clear.

Serpent of Lumina

The Serpent of Lumina is a creature of striking beauty and deadly elegance, its translucent, shimmering scales glowing with an otherworldly light. Its body undulates like liquid silver, and it moves with fluid grace, either gliding through the air or slithering through the water, always silent and mesmerizing. The Serpent's emerald eyes are hypnotic, capable of locking its prey in a trance, rendering them vulnerable to its power.

When the Serpent exhales, glowing spores drift from its nostrils, creating an ethereal glow that dances in the air. These spores have unique properties, capable of calming the fiercest creatures or lulling them into a peaceful stupor. Despite its hypnotic nature, the Serpent of Lumina is a creature of danger, an ancient force whose very presence can alter the course of events. It is a symbol of temptation and control, showing that beauty and danger are often intertwined.

Thunder Wolf

The Thunder Wolf is a majestic and fearsome creature, known for its untamed strength and the electricity that crackles through its fur. Its fur seems to shimmer with energy, glowing softly in the dark, and each of its steps causes the air to hum, charged with static electricity. The Thunder Wolf is a perfect fusion of grace and raw power, with a sleek, muscular body built for speed and agility. Its glowing blue eyes can pierce through the thickest darkness, and its howl can summon storm clouds and thunder to engulf the land.

This creature embodies the raw, untamable forces of nature, commanding respect wherever it roams. Its presence is a reminder of the destructive potential of nature, but also its capacity to renew. The Thunder Wolf is not just a physical force but a creature that seems to be one with the very storms that swirl around it, making it a symbol of nature's unpredictable and uncontrollable fury.

Aether Drake

The Aether Drake is a small but incredibly elusive creature, a dragon-like being whose sleek body shimmers with iridescent scales. Its scales bend the light around it, making the Aether Drake nearly invisible in its environment. It moves with such agility that it often seems to disappear, a mere flicker of light before it vanishes into thin air.

Though small compared to other legendary creatures, the Aether Drake has the power of evasion and confusion. It is capable of moving faster than the eye can track, using its speed to disorient and outmaneuver its opponents. Its cries are hauntingly beautiful, capable of soothing minds and calming anger, yet its roar can freeze even the bravest warriors in their tracks. The Aether Drake represents the beauty of elusive strength—the ability to slip through the world unseen but leaving an impact nonetheless.

Basilisk

The Basilisk is a creature shrouded in myth, feared for its deadly gaze that can turn anyone to stone with a single glance. It is a creature of ancient origin, its very presence a terrifying reminder of the power of legends. The Basilisk's scales are dark and iridescent, reflecting the dim light of its surroundings with an eerie glow. Its eyes—glowing with an unsettling yellow light—hold an almost hypnotic power that can freeze its prey in place, paralyzing them in fear.

Though its gaze is its most feared weapon, the Basilisk is also known for its immense physical strength. With serpent-like grace and agility, it can move silently through the shadows, striking when least expected. The creature's venomous bite can bring death just as swiftly as its gaze. In Phoenix - Ashes and Fury, the Basilisk embodies the dangers of unchecked fear and power—an ancient, lethal force that must be contained.

These mystical creatures are not just elements of fantasy—they are forces of nature, carrying deep symbolism and ancient power. Each one plays a part in shaping the world of Phoenix - Ashes and Fury, and their existence is a constant reminder that power must be carefully managed, for even the most beautiful and awe-inspiring creatures can have a dark side. The path to controlling these forces is a perilous one, but it is a journey the characters must take if they hope to survive the chaos that's about to unfold.

About The Author

Sreeram Hanumanth is a designer and storyteller whose creative journey has always been deeply intertwined with his love for superhero tales and mythic narratives. Over a decade ago, he began shaping his first story, driven by a desire to create a world where extraordinary powers and human struggle collided. Although the project was set aside for years, the story never lost its hold on him.

Three years ago, Sreeram reignited his passion for the script, determined to finish what he had started. **Phoenix - Ashes and Fury** marks the culmination of that dedication, blending his artistic background with his fascination for epic transformations, heroism, and the mythological. As a designer, Sreeram approaches world-building with a unique perspective, making each scene as vivid and immersive as the next.

This book is his first foray into the world of writing, but Sreeram views it as only the beginning. With a deep respect for superheroes, mysticism, and the power of storytelling, he plans to continue expanding his creative universe, inviting readers to join him on a journey full of twists, revelations, and transformation.

When not writing, Sreeram can be found immersed in his design work, drawing inspiration from the world around him.